THIEF OF MY HEART

A BELMONT ROMANCE

NICOLE FRENCH

raglan

For all the first loves

ONE

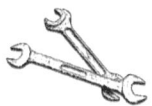

RULES TO GETTING ALONG WITH YOUR NEW BOSS

February 2001

Michael

"Here, you submit your time card. Here, you check your assignments. You do good, I train you to drive the limo, too. Get the tips, eh? Maybe throw you some overtime."

I followed the owner of Zola Auto and Drive as he gave me the ten-minute tour of the shabby little garage. It was nothing special, almost identical to any other body shop in the Bronx. Except this one came with a dedicated corner for restoring classic muscle cars and two eighties-era limousines that probably made the rounds during prom season in the Bronx.

I took in the details: two lifts bearing cars in different stages of repair, a cluttered office near the entry, and rickety stairs leading to a breakroom where

I'd be sleeping for the foreseeable future. This gray box, reeking of motor oil and stale coffee, while a scratched Dean Martin record warbled from the back corner, was my new home.

Maybe "home" was a bit generous. A place to hang my frayed Yankees hat. A garage where I could make a little coin while I figured out what the hell I was going to do with my life now that I'd screwed it up.

Not that I was complaining. The breakroom was already better than most places I'd lived. Hard to beat group homes stuffed with five to a room or a different friend's couch every few days.

Besides, most kids who got out of Rikers ended up in shelters, if not halfway houses, because they couldn't find nothing better. At least I had Father Deflorio, my ma's old priest. He was able to hook me up with a shabby mattress and a part-time job at this shop owned by Mattias Zola, another parishioner. As a newly released parolee, I couldn't ask for much else. I might as well have been walking around with a neon sign over my head reading "Fuck Up."

"Key to the room."

I blinked when a key hooked onto a green rabbit's foot was dangled in front of my nose. I pocketed it with a grunt. "Thanks, Mr. Zola. I appreciate it."

Anyone would know Mattias Zola was Italian to the bone even without hearing that thick accent. It was something innate fewer and fewer residents of Belmont had about them. Dude was old school, the type who always wore a hat when he left the house, still danced with his wife to Rosemary Clooney, and spent his summer afternoons playing cards and sipping espresso with his cronies at the sidewalk cafes lining Arthur Avenue.

He seemed bigger than he actually was, with the kind of shoulders, chest, and hands a guy his size would never get without doing physical labor his whole life. His thick neck strained against the open collar of his polo shirt. Around it gleamed a silver crucifix and San Gennaro medallion, glinting under the shop's fluorescents. His face, with a craggy nose and thick black brows that didn't match his otherwise steely gray hair, wasn't rude or anything. But you could tell he wouldn't put up with your shit.

Zola set a heavy hand on my shoulder. "Call me Mattias. Father Deflorio and me, we're family. It's what family does. It's what we're about here."

I looked doubtfully around the shop and its four mechanics. Family. That was a laugh. I didn't know the meaning of the word, and even if I did, I wasn't going to find it in a car garage.

"Thanks," I said again. Then, out of curiosity, "Naples?"

Zola's dark eyes brightened beneath the brim of his driving cap. "Nineteen fifty-six. Too long ago. You know Napoli?"

I chuckled. "I had a grandpa from there. He came in forty-eight. Lived in Brooklyn, though."

Zola nodded, like I'd passed some kind of test. I didn't tell him that I never met my nonno because he also died less than ten years after arriving in New York, thanks to his involvement with the mob. He wasn't even a made man. Lived just long enough to knock up my grandma before meeting his maker at the bottom of the East River.

Something told me that Zola wouldn't exactly be impressed. From what I could tell, the guy was clean as a fuckin' whistle, and I didn't want to give him any reasons to let me go. He was taking a chance on me as it was.

"We only got the four rules here," he said as he led me back to his office. He took a seat on the torn leather swivel chair behind the desk full of papers and turned down the stereo. "First, you come in on time. Second, you do your work, no trouble. Third, you don't steal."

"And the fourth?" I wondered as I eyed an auto-graphed picture of Frank Sinatra.

Zola—the only man besides me who wasn't dressed in coveralls—pulled meditatively on his suspenders. "Fourth—and most important—you stay away from my granddaughters."

I wondered if he was joking. He *had* to be joking, right? That wasn't a real rule; it was the kind of thing men said in bad comedies or comic books. You couldn't go around telling your employees who they could and couldn't talk to. People didn't do that.

But when I met Zola's gaze, I could tell that he meant business. His beefy hand gestured toward two framed photos on his desk. One was a black-and-white portrait of a dark-haired beauty, a dead ringer for Sophia Loren. His wife, probably, considering the fact that the picture was probably taken sometime in the late fifties or early sixties.

Damn. Mattias Zola had some game back in the day.

The other was blurrier and harder to see, considering it had a lot more people in it. From where I stood, it looked like Zola was sitting in the middle of a bunch of kids—at least five or six.

Grandbabies.

I hid a laugh behind one hand. It wouldn't be the first time someone told me to stay away from their kids (or grandkids, in this case), but not at a job and not with the kind of "fuck around and find out" expression Zola was currently sporting. Did the guy really think I was interested in screwing around with a bunch of little kids?

I wondered, though, if every guy in the shop got that rule tacked on to the list of dos and don'ts or if it was specially reserved for the ex-con charity case.

Not that it mattered. What was I gonna say? No?

"Got it," I said shortly. "No problem."

"Good." Zola handed me a time card and a pen. "Fill this out, and go see Tony under the Chevy. He'll get you a jumpsuit and give you your first assignment."

I took the time card without argument. There was nothing left to say.

Tony, the senior mechanic, was an older man with a thick mustache groomed to perfection. He gave me a nod when I emerged from the bathroom dressed in a pair of grease-stained coveralls that had the name "Stan" embroidered in red over the left breast pocket.

I didn't ask what happened to Stan.

"Take the green Plymouth out for a spin. I just redid the engine, but Mattias wants you to warm her up. After that, she needs a detail before going out to a wedding."

Tony smirked. "If you want, you can write 'Just Married' on the rear window."

I caught the keys. When I didn't say anything, Tony frowned.

"Don't say much, do ya?"

I shrugged and fingered the keys. "Don't have much to say."

"Not even about a seventy-one Barracuda?"

What was he looking for here? Sure, I might have made a big deal out of the fact that sitting in front of me was one of the most hunted muscle cars of its time. I might have been shocked that someone rented it for their wedding instead of a standard Town Car or a Rolls. I might have been amazed at the excellent restoration work that I had a feeling was Tony's.

I might have done…something. But I couldn't.

So I shrugged again, not wanting to set him off. "It's a great car."

Tony seemed to accept it. But as I walked toward the door, I heard him mutter under his breath, "Fuckin' ex-cons."

Sometimes you really can't win.

The 'Cuda was admittedly a beaut. Emerald green, with a bumper that gleamed like it was made of diamonds, even on a cloudy February day.

I slid into the driver's seat, feeling the leather steering wheel under my hands. The last time I'd been in a car was the night before I'd been booked. The second I touched the wheel, I knew it was wrong. I had known, and I'd done it anyway.

Fear hammered through me, sudden and electric.

No. That's not where I was. This was okay. I was

okay. Fuck, I was *more* than okay with my hands on a piece like this, a job, the possibility for some kind of future offered right here. All I had to do was try. All I had to do was take it.

I tightened my grip and started the engine. The car roared to life, banishing my fears, and I backed it out of the garage slowly, trying to get a feel for the way it handled. The Barracuda was a classic car with a lot of power under the hood, big and heavy as it rolled over the concrete.

Inside, though, I felt a little bit lighter.

For the first time in two years, I almost felt like a free man.

BY THE END of the day, I was beat. Every part of my body was sore, unused to hours spent under the hood, the time on my feet, and the pure focus needed to make a car sing. The rhythm was familiar—I hadn't forgotten how to do an oil change or test the brakes or any of the other mundane tasks that Tony kept me on all day. But the simple act of moving all day instead of spending hours in a cell had me aching top to bottom and dying for a bed by the time the shop closed at six.

When I clocked out, I was rewarded by Zola's shock when he discovered that I'd not only detailed the Barracuda, along with the rest of the cars in his fleet, but had fixed a misfiring spark plug when everyone else had left for lunch.

"You found that?" he wondered as I slipped my time

card into its slot. "Tony's been restoring this car for three months and didn't catch it."

I shrugged. "It's easy if you know what to listen for."

"Mmm." Zola gave me a look like he knew I was full of shit. Misfiring spark plugs were hard for even the best mechanics to catch.

But I wasn't going to brag about the fact that I'd disassembled *and* rebuilt engines like that one in half the time it'd taken his top mechanic. Just like he wasn't going to ask me how I learned those particular skills in a chop shop ten blocks from here, and I wasn't going to tell him. I was here for a fresh start and then to move on.

"Good work," Zola said as he took my time card and went to lock up.

I fished the green rabbit's foot out of my pocket and turned toward the stairs leading to the breakroom. "Thanks."

Each step seemed like climbing a mountain. After ten straight hours working, I was ready to get the hell out of these clothes, go to the bodega for a slice, then collapse on the ratty plaid couch in the corner.

Then I opened the door and found myself face-to-face with an honest-to-God angel.

All the aches in my limbs disappeared along with pretty much any other feeling.

Which was fine with me, since the moment I saw her, I couldn't move at all.

TWO

SHE'S DEFINITELY NO ANGEL

Michael

I blinked. Rubbed my eyes. And blinked again.

No, I wasn't hallucinating from hunger or from being too fuckin' tired to see straight. She was still standing there, as real as I was, but a hell of a lot better looking.

Then she gave the cutest little cough I'd ever heard, and I realized that it wasn't a heavenly being that was looking around the breakroom like it belonged to her. Just a really beautiful girl, dressed like every other girl in Belmont, holding a pie pan covered with foil.

She was a little on the shorter side, with dark hair that fell like a waterfall almost to her hips and pointed to the Promised Land, to a perfectly shaped ass. She was wearing a black tank top, an open purple sweater that slid off one of her narrow shoulders, and a pair of tight jeans that hugged her ass so perfectly that I would have sworn God Himself designed them.

She was nice to look at, sure. Okay, better than fuckin' nice.

Which only made her grimy surroundings stand out that much more.

She didn't belong here. Not in this room and sure as shit not with me. Not now. Not ever.

It was funny—while I was in Rikers, I would have killed for a pretty girl like this to be dropped in my lap. But since getting out three weeks ago, I barely knew who I was. How was I supposed to offer that to anyone else?

The door fell shut behind me. The girl startled, then swung around with a glare painted across a face copied straight out of my dreams. High cheekbones, a long nose that gave her what my ma would have called "character," and sharp green eyes the same color as the Barracuda downstairs. They pierced the room like arrows.

"Who are you?" she demanded.

Her tone and words weren't nearly as pretty as the lips that formed them, and just like that, the halo slipped the rest of the way off and shattered.

I wandered to the fridge in search of the PBR I'd bought during my lunch hour with one of the three twenties Father Deflorio shoved into my pocket this morning. Apparently, *that* was what the collection fund was for.

"Name's Mike," I said over my shoulder. "Who the hell are you?"

Normally, I was the cool one in the room. The one with all the control, the one who was never ruffled.

But this girl had me rattled, standing there with her

little pan, hip popped out, surveying me like she was the queen of fuckin' France. Her frown formed an eleven-shaped crease between her brows as she watched me flop onto the couch, crack open my beer, and toss back at least half of it in one go.

She didn't even try to hide her disgust.

So, I tossed out every manner my ma taught me and gave the biggest, loudest burp I could muster.

She didn't disappoint.

"What, not even an 'excuse me'?"

Her voice was unexpectedly husky, like the croon of a tenor sax in a windstorm. It gave the impression that she was almost out of breath. I found myself wondering what that voice would sound like screaming my name. Preferably while I grabbed her hair and took her from behind. Slapped that perfect ass and taught her a lesson in manners.

I kicked off my boots. And then belched again.

The girl recoiled. "You are *disgusting*."

"Maybe," I said. "But a man's allowed to be what-ever the fuck he wants in his own house, princess."

Her mouth, curiously heart-shaped, dropped open. "This isn't your house, asshole. It belongs to my grand-father, in case you forgot on your very first night."

It was like a gavel fell. Somehow heavier than the one that sent me to prison.

I sat up straight. "You're one of Mattias's grand-daughters?"

It didn't make sense. In the picture on his desk, the oldest girls looked like middle-school brats obsessed with Britney Spears. Not this bitchy, holier-than-thou, fully grown, exquisitely filled out…goddess.

Who already hated my guts.

Fuck me.

"This is the breakroom, not your *castle*, you complete and total ogre," she was saying. "I'm looking for my nonno, but he wasn't in his office."

"He left for a job a while ago. I don't know when he'll be back."

Suddenly, I felt a little embarrassed. The contessa here wasn't a bitch. Just a kid doing something nice for her grandpa. Probably bringing dinner to the man who was helping me out when no one else would.

Time to eat crow like the juiciest burger on the planet.

"Sorry about earlier." I stood up quickly, then looked at my hands, which were still covered with smudges of grease, and the top of my coveralls, tied around my waist over a dirty white undershirt. Classy. "I, uh, I'm Mike. Scarrone, that is."

The hell with it. Tentatively, I crossed the room and extended a paw. Anyone else, I would have spared the mess, but this girl was clearly familiar with the garage and everything that came with it. She already thought I was an unmannered slob. The least I could do was present a hand for her to shake.

She looked at it for a long time. Then, to my surprise, she set the pan on the counter and shook it with a surprisingly strong grip.

I tried not to notice the electricity that danced up my tattoo-covered arm. Tried to ignore the hint of rose and sunshine that suddenly seemed to surround me.

I completely fucking failed.

"I'm Lea," the girl said. "And it's fine…Michael.

Nonno doesn't usually let anyone stay here, but I guess he made an exception for you."

I raised an eyebrow—both at the fact that she was using my formal name and at the information about her grandfather. "Why's that?"

Lea's full lips curved upward. The lower one was only a little bigger than the top, and I wanted to suck on it.

"Because you're an ex-con, and he owes Father Deflorio a favor. The priest must like you."

Once again, reality slapped me in the face. So much for moving on from the past. "They told you about me?"

"As in, told me not to talk to you? They did." She shrugged, like directly disobeying my boss and her grandfather was no more consequential than spilling milk. "But I'm a grown woman. I can make my own choices."

I swallowed. I should have told her to listen to her grandpa and go. That he had her best interests at heart. That I had no interest in crossing him or in losing my one chance at getting back on my feet before I'd barely managed to stand upright.

Instead, I nodded. "Oh. Well. I, uh, appreciate it."

Her eyes flickered over me, taking in the tattoos cover both of my arms, the smudges of grease on my hands and face, and the two-day scruff on my chin. I felt like I was being undressed. It was unnerving but not unpleasant.

"What did you do?" she wondered bluntly.

I stiffened. That green-eyed inspection was hard to

read. She was intrigued, maybe. But also a little intimidated.

That's all right, sweetheart. It's probably better for both of us if you're scared.

"I don't think that's any of your business." I took another swig of beer.

She sighed like she was dealing with a little kid and started to unwrap her dish. "I'll find out eventually. We don't keep secrets in our house."

I hoped to God that wasn't true.

"I guess it's not that surprising you're here," she went on. "My nonno does like to take in strays. Feeds them and everything. Drives my grandmother crazy."

She brought the dish to the convection oven in the corner, and I enjoyed another view of her tiny waist and the flare of her perfect, too fucking grabbable ass. It was distracting enough that being compared to a neighborhood mongrel barely bothered me. Jesus.

"Last year, he found a dog under the River Parkway," she said as she put the casserole dish in to warm. "Brought it home. Let it sleep in the living room by the fireplace."

I walked closer and leaned against the counter. She was near enough that I caught another whiff of her perfume—some kind of flowery soap blended with scents of home cooking. Better than anything I'd smelled in a long time.

"He sounds like a stand-up guy," I said. "Guess I'm lucky he's taking a chance on me too. I promise I won't piss on your leg."

I crossed my arms and enjoyed the way her eyes

popped a bit when she stole a look at my biceps. Then she snorted and went back to fiddling with the oven.

I scowled and slid toward her just because I could.

"I wouldn't get too excited," she said. "That dog ran off again two months later. My brother found it back on the Parkway, killed by a driver."

She turned, then started a little when she realized how close we were. Her tits brushed my forearms, nipples slightly visible through her shirt. From this height, I also had a very nice view of her cleavage, which framed a few necklaces, including a cross dangling across her clavicle and another saint's pendant nestled between her breasts.

Lucky motherfucker.

So she was a church girl. No real surprise. Most of the neighborhood was, in one way or another. We all grew up going to Mass with our aunties, taking communion, maybe even going to confession to have our sins forgiven.

Me, I was a long way past forgiveness. But something told me Lea Zola was a little better than the average sinner. She was pure in a way I hadn't seen in a long time.

And God knew I wanted to dirty her up.

She glanced around the room, as if the garbage bag of clothes and empty wallet on the table would tell her something more about me. "Some animals go back to what they came from. Even if it's bad for them."

When she looked back at me, her green eyes felt like darts, and my chest was the bullseye.

She had perfect aim.

I took another thick swallow of beer. Did she think I

was that dog on its way back to where it really belonged? And if that was the case, why didn't she think that place was here? The Bronx was my home.

Wasn't it?

She walked to the door, pausing as she opened it. Her eyes found mine again, bright with something else I recognized. Curiosity. The kind that got good girls like her in trouble with bad men like me.

Fuck, I wanted to invite her to stay.

But Mattias Zola had only given me four rules to follow.

And this here was the most important one.

"I'll let him know he's got dinner when he gets back," I told her.

Lea shook her head. "Don't bother. He'll come home looking for his wife when he's ready to eat. That's for you."

At that, I had nothing to say. Did that mean she had come here with the express purpose of feeding me dinner? Why would she do that for someone she never knew? Someone she had expressly been forbidden to meet? Someone who, for all she knew, was a hardened criminal legitimately capable of doing her harm.

"I—er—"

"Thanks is fine, Michael." Those green eyes dragged down my body so slowly, it set me on fire. "Have a good night."

THREE

EIGHT GIRLS, ONE THING ON THEIR MINDS

Lea

I returned to the little brown house on Hughes Street soon after dark. It wasn't much different from other houses in Belmont, most of them wedged between townhomes and apartment buildings exactly like ours was. It was full of mismatched furniture my grandparents had been collecting since they married in the late fifties, the cream-colored walls scattered with old family portraits, religious iconography, and the occasional "beautiful scene" Nonna sometimes found at the mall and had framed. The wood floors were scuffed, the rugs faded, and there was always a pile of jumbled shoes near the front door.

But it was true home, safe and warm. And considering that I still remembered what it was like not to have one, I was grateful every time I stepped inside.

I hung my jacket on the hooks next to the front door and removed my sneakers before making my way through the living room and down the narrow hall leading to the kitchen and dining room, where I could hear my sisters' ever-present squabbling.

"Was he there?" Nonna asked once she spotted me.

Sofia Cirino Zola was in her favorite place—the kitchen—cleaning up from dinner while three of my younger sisters did homework at the dining room table.

In some ways, my grandmother was as much of a rebel as any of her grandkids when it came to disobeying the head of the Zola household. When Nonno informed us that he was helping Father Deflorio rehabilitate another parolee and that we were under no circumstances allowed to visit the garage until he had ascertained the guy's character, she and I had glanced at each other with the mutual understanding of two rebellious good Samaritans. As soon as Nonno called to let her know he had to chauffeur tonight, she wrapped up a plate of ziti and sent me over to feed the newest stray.

I wasn't afraid. I never was. Father Deflorio wouldn't have sent anyone capable of real harm to the garage, and even if they were, no one would dare harm Mattias Zola's family. Not in Belmont. My grandpa was an institution here.

I rounded the kitchen counter to deliver a kiss to my grandmother's not-yet-wrinkled cheek. Sofia Zola was a black-haired beauty in her youth, and honestly, I couldn't see much of a difference even though she was going to turn sixty later this year. Her hair—still black, even if it was dyed—was never out of place, her nails were always done, and I had never seen her wear sneakers unless she was out walking with friends. On top of her beauty, she did all the things a nice Italian wife was supposed to do: raised her son (and then his children), took everyone to church, cooked up a storm, and loved her husband. My grandpa was a very fortunate man, and so were the rest of us.

The example was a little hard to live up to, though.

"He was there," I said. "His name is Michael. I don't know why Nonno is always so worried. Father Deflorio never sends him anything but pussycats, and this one is no different."

My skin prickled at the lie. I hadn't sensed that Michael Scarrone would ever hurt me. But the way his dark-eyed gaze had raked over my body and left a trail of goose bumps in its wake had felt anything but safe.

"Mimi, gimme that! I want to draw stars this time!"

"No, I need it for my math, though! Otherwise, they'll all be in different colors."

"Please, like that matters. You won't get the answers right anyway."

My sisters took up one end of the oval-shaped dining table on the other side of the room as they scuffled over their homework. It was a familiar nightly scene at the Zola household: six-year-old Joni and seven-year-old Marie bickering over who got to use the pink pen while Frankie, only a few years older, served as the de facto babysitter. Our other sister, Kate, was probably avoiding dish duty in our shared bedroom. The other missing family member was my older brother, Matthew, who only came home to sleep now that he was in college at CUNY and otherwise working full time.

"*Gattinas!*" Nonna barked from the sink. "Joni, wait.

Marie will be done in a few minutes, and then you can use the pink pen after her."

Frankie looked relieved when she spotted me, clearly hoping for some assistance. I shook my head. Frankie was finally old enough to help, so now it was her turn to share the load.

"Let me," I said, gently pushing my grandmother away from the sink. "If we finish by six, you can have a nightcap while Kate and I get the girls to bed."

I pulled on a pair of rubber gloves to scrub the ziti pan while Nonna scoured the stove. It was a nightly routine, helping her like this. We all took turns, but I did it more than the others. I couldn't have said why—maybe as the oldest girl, it sort of felt like my place. It was one way I could give back to them for all they had done over the years.

After our father was killed in a drunk driving accident with our mother behind the wheel, you could say the family was broken. They weren't exactly model parents before that, but after Dad died, Mami checked out for good. Once Nonna caught Matthew and me skipping school to sneak food from her pantry to feed the babies, that was it. She brought us home with her that night, and two weeks later, the courts made it legal after our father went to heaven, our mother to prison. We'd been here ever since.

That was almost six years ago, only six months after Joni was born. Now we had a real family. A whole family.

Did I think my grandparents' house was perfect? No. My nonno couldn't use a vacuum cleaner if his life depended on it, and I was pretty sure he'd never cleaned a single dish. Sometimes, they fought like cats and dogs. And then made up just as loudly when they thought the rest of us were asleep.

But it was a hell of a lot better than some of the other families I saw. Half my friends' parents had never been married. Too many others had never even met one of their parents. We honestly had it pretty good, watching Mattias and Sofia Zola's sweet, old-fashioned love story in this chaotic little house.

How many times had I heard the story of how, in 1957, Mattias Zola had spotted his future wife from across the subway platform, ridden the train with her all the way to Brooklyn, where she worked, and then waited for six hours to escort her back to the Bronx? All to get a few hours with her.

He'd fallen in love at first sight. She'd fallen soon after. And neither of them had ever looked back.

It was a far cry from my parents' story—people I didn't think had ever wanted to fall in love, much less raise a family of eight together. They had met at a similarly young age but had gotten married only after Mami got pregnant with my brother. She was six months pregnant when Nonno dragged his only son down the aisle to do the honorable thing. The other five of us came after, probably the results of more drunken nights where someone was too drunk to remember a condom.

Accidents, all of us—or so my mother would yell when she was too hungover to think straight. Sometimes, she even cursed herself for falling for a no-good lout who would never amount to anything. Daddy tried to get back on the wagon a few times, but he'd always fall off again to appease her. Drink, get pregnant, have another baby, misery, drink. Rinse and repeat until you drink yourself right into an accident where you kill your husband and the couple in the other car, then land yourself in prison for your third DUI and three counts of vehicular homicide.

Not exactly a fairy-tale ending.

Me, I'd never been in love. And if that was what love meant—something that literally killed people—I wanted no part of it.

I was eighteen, five months from graduating high school and hopefully following my brother to college next year. I needed a broken heart to interrupt my plans like I needed a hole in my head.

But that didn't mean I wasn't interested in a little fun. I wouldn't mind someone looking at me the way Nonno looked at his wife whenever she walked into the room. Or someone taking my hand and kissing it, like he still did hers after all these years.

No, I wouldn't mind a little sweetness here and there so long as I didn't have to give my heart away to get it.

"Need any more help?" I asked after toweling dry the pan and putting it away. The rest of the dishes were dry and put away already, and Nonna was almost finished with the stove.

She set down the polishing cloth and clasped my face to hers for a moment before shaking her head.

"You're a good girl," she told me, her thick Roman accent curving around the words. "My good girl. Always here to help. No, I can finish."

"Angie and Linda are up in your room with Kate," Frankie called from the table. "For your study session."

I whirled around. "You didn't think to tell me that when I got home?"

Frankie gave me a smirk, as if to say "you deserved it" for leaving her with the littles.

Brat.

Flipping my hair over my shoulder, I exited the kitchen and dashed up the creaky stairs to Kate's and my bedroom. It was across from the other bedroom that Frankie, Marie, and Joni all shared. Nonno and Nonna were on the bottom floor under the stairs, and Matthew was in the attic—until he moved out, at least. And then I was calling dibs.

That's right. Six kids. Two grandparents. One little house.

Cramped, maybe. But still home.

I found Kate sitting cross-legged on her bed while my best friends, Angelica Fernandez and Linda Esposito, gossiped and arranged study materials across my faded daisy-covered bedspread.

"Finally!" Angie exclaimed. "We've been waiting like a million years."

"More like ten minutes," Linda revised dryly as she flipped through the scholarship packet we'd gotten from the Belmont Prep college counselor.

"Sorry about that. I was helping Nonna in the kitchen." I plopped onto the chair at the little white desk Kate and I shared.

"It's fine," Linda replied. "Kate's been giving us the lowdown about the new mechanic your nonno hired."

I frowned at Kate, who gave a shrug before collapsing back onto her pillows. "They asked where you were," she explained while toying with her sketchbook.

"A *sexy* ex-con mechanic," Angie added. "Mike Scarrone. Yo, you are *so* lucky. Total. Freaking. Hottie. That boy is *so* fine."

I peered at her curiously. "How do you know that?"

"The hot part or the criminal part?" Kate wondered to herself, then shoved her glasses up her nose and went back to sketching when I sent her a look.

"Baby, everyone knows that Mike Scarrone is out and that Father Deflorio set him up with your nonno," Angie rattled on as if Kate hadn't spoken. "It was all anyone could talk about at dance team practice today."

I frowned. "Why would the dance team at Belmont Prep be interested in a mechanic? He's probably, like, ten years older than us."

Linda snorted. "Try three."

I balked. "*Three?*"

For some reason, I'd thought Michael was a lot older than twenty-one. There was a weariness in his eyes that generally came with age and experience. I wondered what had put it there. Then shuddered and decided I didn't want to know.

"Girl, where've you been?" Angie demanded. "Mike *Scarrone*. Gina's ex-boyfriend?"

I slapped at the back of my neck, suddenly feeling like something was crawling on it. "Gina Reyes dated Michael?"

Angie nodded, not even bothering to hide her glee as her gold bamboo hoops swung back and forth. "Ohhhh, yeah. Up until he got locked up, anyway. Then, you know, she was messing with Alex Ramirez for a minute. Her cousin's on dance team too—you know Kylie. Anyway, she would *not* shut up about Mike today. And lemme tell you, girl, Gina's got plans for him. Supposedly, she heard he got out and broke up with Alex with a *page*. Can you believe that?"

"Huh." I inspected my nails, urging my face *not* to flush at the idea of Gina Reyes sinking her two-inch claws into Michael Scarrone.

I didn't say more than that. I didn't need to. Both my friends knew exactly how I felt about Gina Reyes. Gorgeous, blonde, flirty-as-fuck Gina Reyes. The girl half of Belmont Prep had fantasized about since her tits first came in. Including the one and only boyfriend I'd ever had.

Kate, however, wasn't in the loop, considering she was only a sophomore and had started school after Gina had graduated. "Who's Gina Reyes?"

"She don't know?" Linda's big brown eyes widened.

I found a pencil on my desk that urgently needed to be sharpened. "There's nothing to know."

Linda snorted, and Angie said, "Okay, then."

"No, really," Kate pressed, sitting up straight and setting her sketchbook on her nightstand. "What did she do?"

I sighed and turned back around to face everyone. "Do we really have to tell this story?"

Angie leaned forward, her eyes bright with excitement. "Yes, we do."

I rolled my eyes but began anyway. "If we must. You, um, remember Victor Jenkins?"

Every girl in the room nodded—my two best friends, plus Kate, knew everything about my first and only boyfriend. They knew Victor was the point guard for Belmont Prep's basketball team two years ago. They knew we'd met at one of his games when I'd caught the ball in the stands. They knew he'd pursued me for weeks, told me he loved me, promised me I would be his girl.

"Well, we almost..." I trailed off. I couldn't quite bring myself to say it in front of my little sister. Like it would make me a bad influence, even if she was plenty old enough to know about sex and everything else teenagers do.

"Did the bad thing?" Kate provided unhelpfully. "At his senior prom? And then went to confession every day for a week after?"

I shot her a glare. "*You* aren't supposed to know about that."

Kate wasn't particularly fazed. "Then *you* shouldn't leave your diary where anyone could find it."

"It was under my mattress!" I scowled, making my friends giggle.

"That's amateur hour, Sis. You've learned since then."

I glared but couldn't argue with her. There was a small safe under my bed to prove it, containing my current journals, a pair of gold earrings, and the necklace that had once belonged to my mother's grandmother. I'd saved for a year to buy myself some measure of privacy in this house full of people.

"*Anyway*," I said meaningfully. "I was only fifteen. A little young to be giving it up after a few months, don't you think?"

Angie just shrugged, and Linda looked away. Both

of them had lost theirs years ago. Meanwhile, I was still practically the angel in white.

Not that I was ashamed.

"Whatever," I said. "I had bigger plans than some boy, and I still do. But back then, well, Victor distracted me for a while."

"Until Gina found out," Linda added.

Kate looked back at me. "She was with him too?"

"She wanted to be," Angie filled her in. "Everyone did. And it was before she went out with Mike Scarrone. Apparently, after Lea turned him down at prom, Victor heard that Gina would put out. So he took her to the hotel and left Lea at the dance."

Kate's jaw dropped. "Le, you didn't tell me that!"

I frowned, staring at my hands. I needed a manicure, but I wasn't going to get another shift helping with Nonno's books until Michael was out of the picture. "You were a little young to be hearing about that kind of stuff."

"It didn't end there, though," Linda said. "Victor tried to run back to you. Even after you turned him down, Gina made your life a living hell for the next year. Spread rumors. Told everyone you were frigid and shit. Gave you that horrible nickname."

"What nickname was that?" Kate asked.

I hid my reddened face and mumbled something into my jacket sleeve.

"What?" my sister asked again.

I released the sleeve. "Cherry Popper," I muttered, my face heating up even more.

Kate's eyes widened in shock before she burst into laughter. "Oh my God, that's horrible!"

"It doesn't even make sense!" I exploded. "It was *my* cherry that hadn't been popped. I wasn't going around popping others! And honestly, how do you even pop a cherry? It's a piece of fruit, not a bubble."

Angie and Linda started giggling with Kate, and I couldn't help but join in. It was ridiculous, really. But the fact remained that the idea of Gina Reyes had loomed over me for years. It shouldn't bother me that she was the uncouth (and yes, ridiculously fine, smoking *hot*) new mechanic's ex-girlfriend. Just like it shouldn't have bothered me that she apparently wanted him back.

But it did. It really did.

"So, what are you going to do about it?" Linda wondered once the laughter had died away.

I shrugged. "Why would I do anything? I don't have any claim on the guy. Or any interest, for that matter."

Straight-up lies. I was going to be in confession for hours this Sunday.

"Mami, please," Angie put in as she studied her bright pink acrylics. "You turned red the second we brought him up. I remember what Mike Scarrone looks like. Like that bad boy in *American Beauty*, but with muscles. And tattoos." She cocked her head. "At least I think Mike has tattoos."

"He has tattoos," I confirmed, neglecting to mention how many there were or that I'd wondered how much of his body they covered.

I couldn't, however, ignore the way my skin tingled at the memory of his sleeves of ink. His coveralls had been tied around his waist, and he wore a stained white tank on top that did nothing to hide the wiry muscles rippling underneath the thin cotton, where the winding designs covering his arms from knuckle to neck disappeared.

I had busied myself in the tiny kitchenette just to stop from staring. Between the body art, the five o'clock shadow matching his dark brown hair, the lightly tanned skin smudged with grease, and the soulful brown eyes...one thing was for sure. Michael Scarrone wasn't one of these *boys* who had broken my heart. He was one hundred percent man.

And that felt more exciting and more dangerous than any crime he may have committed.

I shook the memories away. I couldn't afford to be distracted by pretty, dangerous men.

"Even if I was interested, I have too much going on. Starting with studying for this damn test." I pulled my own packet from the backpack on the floor and set it on the desk with a loud smack. "We aren't here to gossip, babies. College applications are in, and Mama wants a scholarship. So let's get to work."

A FEW HOURS LATER, after Angie and Linda had left and Kate and I had finally gotten our sisters to sleep, we crawled into our own beds. On the other side of the wall, I could hear the murmurs of my grandparents before they went to sleep too. Matthew had arrived thirty minutes ago, carried a plate of leftovers to the attic, and disappeared for the night.

We had just turned out the light, and I was trying to close my eyes when Kate spoke.

"It's okay if you're a virgin, you know."

I flipped over on my pillow so I could see her pale face across the darkened room. "Um, I know."

"I'm just saying. It's fine."

I traced a finger over my bedspread. "Well, someone has to set a good example for the rest of you."

Kate didn't laugh at my feeble joke. "You're eighteen. I don't think you need to worry about that for the littles. Certainly not for me. Not anymore."

"What does that mean?"

She shrugged. "That's it's not a big deal. At least, it wasn't for me."

I was stunned into silence. I wasn't angry that my little sister wasn't exactly a girl anymore. Kate was cute, and at sixteen, she was old enough to make her own choices. And even though she was still working through her awkward phase, she was pretty. None of the Zola kids were bad-looking.

Maybe what really surprised me was that it happened for her before it had for me.

"Who?" I asked, propping my head up with one hand. "You never said anything about a boyfriend."

Kate's cheeks undoubtedly pinked in the dark.

"Tyler Kim," she offered. "Definitely *not* my boyfriend. It happened after we stayed late one night to strike the set for *My Fair Lady*. His parents were at work."

Never an actress, Kate worked on a lot of theater productions put on at Belmont Prep. This, however, was the first time I'd heard of her getting involved with anyone there.

"A theater kid?" I ventured, trying to place the name to a face. "Really?"

"He builds the sets. I stayed to help even though I did costumes. He has nice arms."

"So…you gave it up because you liked someone's biceps?"

"No." Kate sighed. "I wanted to know what it was like, I guess. Figured I should get it over with, and Tyler is a nice guy who won't blab my shit all over Belmont, you know?"

I opened my mouth to say that making the safe choice isn't how most girls would go about giving up their virginity, but then I realized I couldn't really talk. I was prioritizing the safe route myself. Maybe too safe.

"Okay," I said carefully. "Cute. I guess." I honestly didn't know what more to add. "How was—" I swallowed back my question. I wasn't really sure I wanted all the details on Kate's sex life. But she was my sister, after all. I needed to ask something. "Was it all right? Were you…all right?"

After a moment more, she answered. "I'll probably do it again. Just not with him."

I swallowed. There were other things I wanted to know, but it suddenly felt weird to pressure my sister in a way I never had before. Why wasn't she interested in Tyler? Had it hurt a lot? Was it awkward? Had he treated her all right after? I supposed the fact that she was willing to do it again meant it wasn't so bad. But if not with that guy, then who?

"I feel bad for him," she whispered before I could figure out my next question.

"Who, Tyler Kim?" I asked. "I don't know why. He was probably walking on clouds after that."

"No, not Tyler. The guy in Nonno's shop."

"Michael?"

I don't know why I said it that way. Calling him Michael instead of Mike, the way my friends had. But I kept seeing those dark eyes smirking at me, masking a deeper hurt that I wanted to fix more than anything.

"Yeah," Kate murmured.

"Don't tell me you have a thing for tattoos too."

Kate gave a snort. "Not like your friends. I only mean...he must be lonely. Two years in prison. Now he's living in a breakroom over a garage. It means he has no one; otherwise, he would have had somewhere to go."

For the second time that night, my sister left me speechless. This time, it wasn't because I couldn't think of anything to say—but because there were too many thoughts racing through my head.

Like wondering where Michael had come from if his only refuge was my grandpa's garage.

Whether Michael had enough to eat after he was finished with the ziti.

If Nonno left on the heat or if Michael's clothes would keep him warm through the night.

I turned toward the window. Flakes of snow were starting to fall, evident only in the glow of a streetlight a few houses down.

I was used to the constant noise of New York. The hints of music blaring from apartment buildings and nearby restaurants. The huff and squeal of the buses on Crotona Avenue. The chatter of people making their way to and from the restaurants on 187th.

Normally, it all wooed me right to sleep, but tonight,

I found myself staring toward the hum while Kate's breathing grew deeper.

Shadows flickered outside my window as people walked past.

I wondered if one of them was Michael Scarrone.

I wondered if he was all right.

FOUR

A GHOST CAN BE A PUNK TOO

Michael

My second day on the job went about the same as the first. The garage opened at eight, which meant I rolled off the breakroom couch with a sore neck at seven fifty. I tugged Stan's coveralls over another dollar-store undershirt, tromped downstairs with my boots still untied, slugged back some shitty coffee in the office, and clocked in under Zola's watchful eye.

I half wondered if he would ask how the ziti was or why in the fuck I had spoken to his granddaughter instead of leaving the premises as soon as I realized who she was. But he was too busy reviewing invoices to do more than nod at my sleepy hello and the dish I set on his desk. Either he didn't know how the ziti had ended up in my stomach, or he didn't care. I wasn't going to push my luck.

I spent most of the day working on the engine of a '78 Caddy that belonged to a young hood who needed a way out of town fast. I knew the look. I'd worn it more than once myself. There were enough gangsters left in this part of the Bronx that even the tourists on Arthur Avenue still blended with a boss or two and their lackeys.

This guy arrived at eight sharp, handed Zola a wad of cash, and begged us to get him on the road tomorrow, no matter the cost. He was desperate. And as much as I hated to admit it, I saw a little of myself in him. Enough that it would feel damn good to have the engine purring like a kitten when I handed him back his keys.

If I couldn't get out, at least I could help someone else on their way.

I had to admit, though, it felt good to earn like an honest man for once. I was good with cars, which gave me the perfect distraction from my nonexistent bank account and lack of official residence. It almost stopped me from checking the goddamn door every time the bell rang to see if Lea Zola was back with another casserole.

Almost.

Honest to fucking God, though. I'd met the girl for all of ten minutes, and I could not get her out of my head. The way her perfect mouth smirked when she thought she knew better than me. Or the way her perfect ass swayed when she turned around. Or the way her perfect tits would feel under my palms and how she might squeak when I copped a feel between her—

Fuck. Me.

I really had to stop.

Luckily, Zola ran a tight operation that didn't leave much time for illicit daydreaming about his granddaughter. The guys respected him, but his grease monkey days were behind him, so he kept separate from us, either in his office or else out driving clients. The shop was known and trusted by everyone in the neighborhood, from the moms looking for a quick oil change to the bosses who needed someone to fix the finish on their Lincolns. Zola walked the tightrope well—the man might have worked for everyone, but he belonged to no one.

Men like that aren't the ones to cross.

"Mike? Is that Mike fuckin' Scarrone I see?"

I was seven minutes into my mid-morning break, enjoying a second cigarette outside the front entrance, when I saw Paul Reyes striding down the sidewalk, yanking up his baggy jeans with one hand and shoving two pedestrians out of his way with the other. One of them was even pushing a stroller.

"You all right?" I asked the stroller woman.

She just kept walking like the wind was carrying her, though she shot Paul a nasty look as she passed us. He didn't notice her at all.

"Scarrone, what the fuck?" he shouted as he held out a hand for me to slap. "Good to see you, man, so fuckin' good. I heard you got out last week."

He still sort of jumped around when he spoke. Paul was a little frog of a guy, always hopping around bigger men, waiting to catch their flies. I didn't like the guy. I never had.

"Who told you?" I flicked my cigarette in the gutter and crossed my arms to ward against the cold. It had snowed a little last night, but everything had melted by morning. Still cold as fuck out here, though. Especially without a jacket.

Paul didn't slow down. "Word gets around."

He threw an arm around my shoulders, which wasn't easy since I was probably six inches taller than the guy.

"Word does." I shook his arm off. "Don't let it get to your head."

This was the last thing I needed. I hadn't told anyone I was out. No one was waiting for me when I left Rikers. No one knew I was coming back to the neighborhood for a lot of reasons, and Paul Reyes embodied every one of them.

"How the fuck are you?" The dude really couldn't take a hint. "Because I know you're not fuckin' my sister. Gina ain't heard from you once. You know she cried every day you were locked up?"

I ground my teeth at his comments. One, I know *that* wasn't true. Two, this was how he talked about his own family?

Not that I was feeling all that gracious toward Gina. My ex—if you could even call a girl you used to hit up every so often an ex—hadn't even had the grace to break up with me properly when I was pinched. Straight-up ghosted me. Not even a letter to the prison.

"I'm not doing anything with your sister," I replied curtly. "Not now, not ever. And you can tell her I said that."

Paul flashed a grin. "I'm joking, guy. Gina's a slut anyway, so no harm, no foul. I just don't want her jawing my ear off about it, you know?"

Real charmer, this guy. Fuck it, I was having another cigarette.

"Zola got some fine-ass granddaughters, though, so at least you got a little eye candy working with you," Paul rattled on while I lit the third smoke of my break. "You remember Matt Zola, their older brother? Dude always thought he was smarter than fuckin' everyone."

"That's because he is," I said. "Kid used to get straight As in every class I had with him."

Before I dropped out, anyway. Matthew Zola was one of those kids everyone loved to hate. The girls all thought he was hot, and the guys who weren't green with envy wanted to be him. But you couldn't actually hate him because he was a genuinely good guy.

No doubt Matt was flying through college at this point. And good for him. He put in the work. He deserved it.

"His sister, though..." Paul was saying.

I grunted. "Which one?"

"Lea Zola. Eighteen, barely legal, and fine as *fuck*."

I grunted again. I was not interested in talking about Lea Zola with this piece of shit.

Paul wasn't getting the vibes, though.

"I saw her at the bodega the other day, and, I mean, damn. Girl grew right up. She got this waist and this ass that looks like she wants to be turned right over and have a real man—"

"That's enough," I snapped. "Her grandpa is on the other side of this door. Have some fuckin' respect."

Paul just laughed. Almost as if he enjoyed the fact that his insults might be overheard.

"I wouldn't bother with her, though," he said. "She's a real ballbreaker."

I scowled. "The fuck does that mean?"

"You should have heard her at the bodega. Got super pissed because her chicken cutlet was a little cold. Had the dude remake it and everything." He shook his head. "If my woman talked to me like that, I'd show her the back of my hand You can tell she's bossy. Fuckin' frigid."

My left hand flexed and fisted, and I had to hold myself back from punching Paul Reyes in the face for even *thinking* about hurting Lea.

A scowl was probably permanently carved into my face by now. I didn't know Lea Zola. She probably was bossy, but if you grew up in this neighborhood, with men like Paul Reyes making comments like that, who could blame her for growing a backbone? Not me. And I definitely knew she was the furthest thing from frigid. The girl was hotter than sin.

The real question was: why did I care what anyone said about her?

"Anyway, Sly Ricky was very curious about what you been doing," Paul continued. "He said Antoni was asking about you too."

My gaze flickered to him as I blew out some smoke. Now we were getting to it. "Lis or Ares?"

Paul grinned, showing two gold crowns. "You know which one."

Fuck. I'd heard about Lis Antoni, the newest boss and de facto head of the Mancuso crime family, now that they'd merged with the Albanian mob in the area.

"He's gonna be very interested to know that you're

working at Zola's garage. Mancuso's been trying to get in here for years. Nice, man. Very nice."

I took a long pull on my cigarette, then exhaled another cloud of smoke. "It's a job. Glad to be out. Working."

"As a driver?" Paul asked hopefully.

The little fucker. Like I hadn't seen what he—and, by extension, Lis Antoni—wanted from a mile away. Drivers were premium lackeys for the mob. They provided trunk space, made it easy to smuggle shit across the region when cars were being towed or dropped off, not to mention they gave the perfect cover for a boss looking to funnel money. While it was possible that Mattias Zola was already on the take, I seriously doubted it if Paul was approaching me like this. And I hadn't seen a single sign of any cars being ripped up for parts.

Being the only honest mechanic left in Belmont was quite a reputation to uphold. It also made Zola a very valuable commodity to acquire.

"No driving," I said shortly. "Repair only." I glanced at him sideways. "And the garage is full, so don't even think of dropping anything off. They don't chop shit up here."

"Anyone can do anything," Paul said with a bright, froggy smile pasted across his wide mouth. "Given the right motivation."

"I don't think so." Suddenly, I was done with the conversation. I took two long pulls on my cigarette, then flicked it into the gutter with the other discarded butts. "I gotta get back to work."

Paul's beady eyes narrowed as I made for the door

without saying so much as goodbye. "So that's how it's gonna be?"

I turned to face him and drew up to my full height. I wasn't huge, but at almost six feet, I was taller than most in this neighborhood, and I could tower over a shrimp like Paul, who was fully aware that I could more than hold my own in a fight.

He tried not to look scared. And failed miserably.

"Yeah, that's how it's gonna be," I informed him. "Tell Ricky and Antoni or Mancuso that I'm straight now. I did my time, didn't rat on anyone, and now I'm out. That was the agreement, Paul. I'm out."

Paul shook his head. And then he chuckled. That motherfucker outright laughed before he shoved me against the wall and put his mouth next to my ear in a fucked-up parody of a kiss. I would have pushed him away if I didn't feel the blunt edge of a knife pressed against my gut.

"What, you think it was by accident that you didn't come out of Rikers with that ass stretched like taffy?" he asked, breath hot with stale menthols. "You owe Rick and the rest of them, Mikey. And I was sent here to say that you *will* pay your debt."

"Or else what, you gonna stab me right here, right now?" I sneered. "In front of the cameras and every-thing? Go ahead and try it, Paulie. We both know I could kick your ass, knife or no."

We both looked up to the security cameras installed over the garage.

"What's the problem here?"

Immediately, Paul released me. He tucked his knife back into his pocket as the door to the garage opened and Mattias Zola walked out, followed by Tony and another mechanic, Juan.

A real fuckin' party.

"Nothing, *Signor* Zola," Paul said with a smile that revealed at least two more fillings. "Just catching up with my old friend Mike here. For old time's sake, yeah?"

Zola's shrewd gaze passed over the two of us, then landed back on me. "Scarrone, I'm not paying you to gossip. Break's over. Back to work."

"No problem." With another glare at Paul, I headed back into the garage.

"See you soon, Mike," he called.

I held up a finger before the heavy door shut behind me. And not the nice one.

My boss caught me right before I slid back under the Caddy.

"Michael."

I sat up. "Yeah, Mr. Zola?"

He squatted beside me, surprisingly limber for a man his age. He stroked his closely shaved chin as he looked me over. Appraising me.

What he saw, I couldn't tell.

"Mattias," he said finally. "You can call me Mattias, remember?"

I nodded, a little nervous. "Mattias. All right, sure."

"That Reyes," he said, jerking his head toward the door as if Paul was still on the other side listening in. "He's your friend?"

I was glad that I could shake my head, and not because saying yes would have been an obvious mark against me. The gleam in Mattias's eye told me he had expected me to say no. It also made me wonder if the cameras outside were equipped with microphones. And how much of the conversation Mattias had overheard.

"Definitely not," I said, and then decided on honesty. I meant it when I said I was going straight. "We used to run together sometimes before I was locked up. But now...no, sir. I don't want nothing to do with him anymore. I was telling him that when you came out."

His thick black brows rose in response. Mattias studied me a moment more, then stood back up. "He come back around and bother you, you let me know, yes?"

I sighed. I definitely wasn't going to do that. But it was nice to know he cared.

"Don't worry about me," I said before I slid back under the car. "He won't come around here again."

A few moments later, someone tapped me on my boot. I slid back out and found Mattias still standing there, arms crossed in thought.

"Need something else, Mr. Zo—er, Mattias?" I asked.

He tipped his head and seemed to make a decision. "You'll come to dinner tonight. My wife, she's making manicotti. Very good. Better than you get anywhere else."

Considering that, other than last night's ziti, every meal I'd had since getting out consisted of grocery store slices and canned oranges, I had no doubt that was true.

But I wasn't an idiot. This wasn't dinner; it was some kind of test. Of what, I didn't know, but one I couldn't fail if I wanted to keep working here. I did know it would mean I'd be breaking bread with my boss, his wife, and his grandchildren—one of whom I'd been thinking some very indelicate thoughts about over the last twenty-four hours.

"I—you don't need to—" I started to protest, but before I could get the words out, my stomach interrupted with a massive grumble.

Mattias looked at my stomach, then back to my face, and rolled his eyes.

"Dinner," he repeated. "You'll come. Tonight, seven o'clock. *Capisce?*"

FIVE

LOOK WHO'S COMING TO DINNER

Lea

"Someone answer the door."

Nonno's raspy voice was gentle while he poured himself a grappa from the brass drinks cart in the dining room.

He gestured vaguely with his glass. "We have company for dinner."

I set the platter of spinach-filled manicotti in the center of the table, where the rest of my siblings had already taken their seats. Now that I was looking, I noticed an extra place set tonight. The most likely candidates for dinner on a Friday were Tino, Nonno's best friend, or maybe one of Nonna's Bible study pals, like Sandra Gomez or Alessia Piras. My grandparents still kept a close circle of the old guard within a few blocks of Arthur Avenue. Any one of them meant a lot of entertainment.

"I got it," I called as I skipped toward the door,

hoping it was Tino. He always brought a pan of tiramisu from his restaurant.

It was definitely not Tino. Instead of a beefy, sixty-something Italian cook, a lean, dark-haired Michael Scarrone was toeing a boot into the doormat while examining fingers that looked like they'd been scrubbed raw.

In fact, most of him looked like he'd made a considerable effort to clean up before arriving on my doorstep. His dark hair was washed and combed to one side, revealing a gold stud in his left earlobe. Yesterday's stained coveralls had been traded for a clean, if faded, black wool coat, dark denim jeans, and boots that were well-worn but had clearly been polished recently.

When he looked up, his eyes were as dark as the shiny leather, fringed with lashes that almost made him look like he was wearing makeup. A flush crept steadily up my neck as he took in the purple knit dress I was wearing. It was church-decent, down to my knees, covering my shoulders and neckline, but somehow felt extremely revealing under that sooty black gaze.

"Hey, Lea. Ah, your grandpa invited me for dinner."

The sound of his voice, low and rough, snapped me out of my daze. "You remembered my name."

Those inky eyes sparked. "Of course I remembered your name. I know all about you and your sisters and brother. Your grandpa showed me your pictures the day I started. He's proud of you."

My mouth opened and closed. I didn't know what to say to that. Of course Nonno would have shown my photo to Michael. All his drivers and mechanics knew us kids on sight, considering our pictures wallpapered his tiny office.

Michael shoved one hand into his pocket in a move so bashful and at odds with his powerful physique that I couldn't help but want to hug him. "Anyway, he invited me for dinner. I, uh, brought this."

Awkwardly, he held out a paper bag crumpled around what was obviously a bottle of wine. The neon green price sticker was still on the screw-top. Three dollars, probably from the bodega. Cheap, but likely all he could afford.

I took it and discreetly pulled off the sticker while Michael removed his coat. My grandparents wouldn't care about the tag—Nonno bought all his wine whole-sale from Tino's restaurant anyway—but Michael already seemed nervous. I didn't want him to be embarrassed about anything. Not when he was so obviously trying to make a good impression.

I couldn't, however, *quite* stop myself from staring when he turned around in a clean, if slightly wrinkled, white button-down with the sleeves rolled up to reveal the tattoos slithering down his powerful forearms. He'd even put on a tie, albeit one that hadn't been tied very neatly.

Cleaned up, yes. But not even close to tame. The combination looked really, really good.

Before I could help myself, I set the wine on the sideboard, then popped up onto my tiptoes to straighten the knot in his tie.

Michael jumped at the sudden close contact.

I shivered.

He smelled like soap and mild cologne and a little

bit of motor oil. None were unfamiliar scents, but on him, together? They were disturbingly delicious.

"Hold still, it's crooked." I pulled at the gray paisley, all too conscious of the minty scent lingering on his warm breath. He'd brushed his teeth right before coming here. For some reason, the idea was endearing.

Our guest morphed into a statue while I took a bit too long to fix his tie. And stare at the St. Gennaro tattoo on the side of his neck. The one that matched the medallion I wore almost every day.

I swallowed. "There, that's better. Nonna likes things neat."

Michael coughed. I thought maybe his cheeks were slightly pinked, but under his stubble, it was hard to tell. "I—Thanks. I guess."

"Anything for her."

I should have stepped away. But I couldn't. And apparently, neither could he. We both stood there, toes maybe an inch apart, breathing each other's scents, staring into each other's eyes. The sounds of my jabbering family, scents of Nonna's manicotti, and glimmers of hallway lights all seemed to fade. For a split second, my entire world revolved around his oddly wizened yet electrically tentative dark-eyed gaze.

And the way it dropped to my mouth. And stayed there.

Holy crap. So, *this* was what they called chemistry.

"Whoa," I whispered before I could help myself.

"Yeah." Michael's voice was suddenly rough. "I—"

"Lea, let the boy in," Nonno called from behind me. He came through the hallway, then set a heavy hand on my shoulder to pull me out of Michael's reach. "Don't crowd him."

Michael hopped back like he'd been bitten, then offered a sheepish smile as I stepped out of the way to let the two of them shake hands.

"Thanks for having me…Mattias," Michael said.

My brows jumped. To his employees, Nonno had always been Mr. Zola or Signor Zola, or maybe Mr. Z if they were on really good terms. The fact that Michael had thrown "Mattias" out there—and that Nonno had let him—told me two things. One, the dude had some balls. And two…Nonno might have actually liked him.

Curious.

"You did good this week," Nonno said to Michael. "Genius with the Barracuda. And you fixed the brakes on the Cabriolet in no time. Faster than Tony. Where did you learn?"

Another notable difference. Nonno wasn't exactly quick with praise.

"I, uh, learned some stuff as a kid at one of the houses where I stayed—the owner was into cars. And then I guess I just picked up things here and there wherever I went. It was one of the few things I was ever good at."

My pulse kicked up as Michael's shoulder brushed mine. Even though it was the briefest touch, he was still warm and solid. He glanced over his shoulder toward me, then followed Nonno as my grandfather chattered about more car repairs.

I followed them back into the dining room, where Nonna had put out the rest of the meal family style.

"Good, good," she said as I handed her the wine. "We needed some."

"It's from our guest, Michael," I told her loudly so everyone would hear.

"*Grazie*, Michael," Nonna said as she offered him a kiss on each cheek, then went back to the kitchen while Nonno introduced the rest of the family after he sat down.

"This is Joni, the baby," Nonno said, gesturing to the two hellcats—otherwise known as my littlest sisters—sitting against the wall. "Marie, next. Frankie over here with Kate. That's Lea helping her grandmother—she answered the door—and Matthew, my grandson, on my right."

"Hi." Michael gave an awkward wave as he lowered himself into the chair on Nonno's other side, clearly overwhelmed by the six Zola kids giving him identical green-eyed stares. He didn't even seem to notice when I slipped into the seat next to his.

"Scarrone, hey," Matthew greeted him. "Heard you were back."

My big brother was as lanky and churlish as you'd expect a twenty-year-old to be. Especially one that had been raising his little sisters for most of his life. But his eyes were as sharp as our grandfather's, and even in the last year and a half, I'd watched Matthew blossom from a boy into a man in the smallest of ways.

"Hey, Matt," Michael said as he reached across the table to bump fists with Matthew. "Good to see you, man."

My brother's eyes flashed quick and bright over Michael, landing on the tattoos, the earring, the broad shoulders. I couldn't tell if the expression was envious or protective. Or maybe a little of both.

"Are you a bad man?" Joni interrupted.

"Joni!" I hissed. "You can't ask people things like that."

She just shrugged. "Why? He has tattoos on his neck and arms. Nonno says only bad man mess their bodies up like that. So I wanted to know."

"*Dai, civetta!*" snapped Nonno, then rattled off a bunch of Italian most of us could only half-understand but knew it didn't bode well for later all the same.

"Don't be dumb," Marie said, shoving Joni's side. "He wouldn't be here if Nonno thought he was a bad man."

"Plus, it's rude," Frankie said from Joni's other side.

"Sorry," Joni mumbled, then turned her water glass around a few times before dipping her finger into it.

"I kind of like them," Kate said from the other side of the table. "The lady right there is pretty."

Everyone immediately studied the tattoo of a woman who looked like she was praying on Mattew's wrist.

"I agree," I murmured, mostly to myself. She *was* pretty, in a saintly sort of way.

Michael's gaze flickered back to me as he reached for a glass of water and pulled the arm in question under the table. "Thanks."

My cheeks heated as I caught my brother's sharp gaze, now following *me*.

I stuck my tongue out at him. Very adult, I know. But he could take the brotherly concern and shove it.

"Lea, come bring the salad," Nonna called from the kitchen.

I sprang up, eager to escape both men's pensive stares.

"So, Matt—or is it Matthew now?" I heard Michael say.

"Mattie," Joni corrected him. "Nobody calls him Matthew but our grandparents."

"Mattie?" Michael seemed less than convinced.

"Matt's fine," Matthew replied in a deeper voice than usual. "She's right. The only people who use my full name are these two."

He gestured toward Nonno and Nonna as she carried in a platter of green beans, then took her seat at the table. I set down the salad and some bread rolls, made sure everyone had napkins and then slid back into my seat next to our dinner guest. Not that he seemed to notice.

"*Benedici*," Nonno announced, folding his hands in front of him and bowing his head.

Obediently, all the Zolas followed suit. Out of the corner of my eye, I saw Michael glance around before mimicking the same movements. His gaze, however, landed on me and stayed there. It was everything I could do not to look up.

We waited while Nonno recited a brief blessing for the table, then obediently all repeated, "Amen."

Then, the table descended into its predictable chaos.

"No, Nonna! I wanted more cheese, not the spinach part."

"Ew! Not this salad again! I told you, I don't like the peppers!"

"Only one roll, *tesoro*. There is more than enough for everyone."

"Pass the green beans. And Mattie, don't hog them, will you?"

By the time everyone was dished up and digging in, Michael still had an empty plate. But only I noticed.

"Do you want some?" I pointed at the hot platter of manicotti.

Michael jerked, then looked at me like he'd only just remembered I was there. "I—sure. Yeah, thank you. It looks great, Mrs. Zola," he said to Nonna.

He held out his plate while I dished him up, doing my best to ignore the trickles of electricity shooting up my arm. I had goose bumps from the simple act of spooning pasta onto his plate.

What was wrong with me?

"Lea, she's my good girl," Nonno said after Michael took his first bite. "Always here to help."

Michael glanced at me with a smirk. I offered a wry smile in return. I knew my grandparents meant well, but it wasn't exactly the sexiest thing in the world, always being called their "good girl."

But I didn't care if Michael Scarrone thought I was sexy.

Right?

"And Matthew, he's in school," Nonno continued, gesturing with his fork. "Very smart, this boy."

"I remember that from back in the day," Michael offered. "You were always first in our classes."

Matthew's green eyes landed squarely on Michael with an appraising expression. "I don't remember you staying in them too long."

Under the table, I kicked my brother squarely in the shin.

"Ow!" Matthew grunted, then mouthed "fuck off" at me.

I mouthed "be nice" right back and kicked his foot again. What was his problem?

Beside me, Michael just looked confused.

"Matthew always gets the straight As," Nonno bragged like there wasn't a cage fight happening directly in front of him.

"Not this semester, Nonno," Matthew replied, as he forked a bit of his pasta. "Calculus is kicking my ass."

"Bah, you'll get it," Nonno told him with a genial clap on his shoulder. "You always do. Genius, my boy here."

"What about you, Mike?" Matthew wondered before shoving a bite of manicotti into his mouth. "You going back to school?"

I tried to kick him again, but this time, he moved his feet, and my shoe hit the rug with a thump.

Matthew grinned after swallowing his pasta, fully aware he was being an overprotective ass. Everyone in the house already knew that Nonno had agreed to take on an ex-con—and if Matthew knew Michael from high school, he certainly knew he wasn't going to college. I honestly wasn't sure if he'd even graduated high school.

All things that should have deterred me completely from my curiosity, but for some reason, were having zero effect.

"I—no. I'm not." Michael's voice was quiet, but he didn't look away from my brother.

"Mattie, don't be a dick," I finally said before winking at Michael. "And, you, don't pay attention to him. He's nothing but a dog who needs a place to pee."

"Says who?" Matthew demanded.

"Says that sad mustache you've been trying to grow on your upper lip for the last month," I retorted. "It looks like dirt. Like you need to wash your face."

"You at Fordham?" Michael asked before my brother could snap back at me. He accepted the green beans Kate passed across my plate, causing her to flush about ten shades of scarlet.

"CUNY," Matthew corrected him before he dished himself some more pasta. "Actually, I was thinking of dropping out. Not sure anymore that college is for me."

The sound of five forks and knives falling onto Nonna's chipped Fiestaware was as deafening as a grenade. It was followed by a raw silence that might as well have been another grenade. Silence wasn't exactly a common occurrence in the Zola household. But Matthew had just dropped a genuine bomb.

SIX

BIG BROTHER TAKES THE HEAT

Lea

"Matthew…" Nonna's voice was a heated whisper.

At the head of the oval-shaped table, Nonno had frozen in his seat. Beside him, Matthew simply stared at his plate, holding his shoulders in an unnaturally upright posture. He was clearly forcing himself *not* to meet our grandfather's imperious stare or shrink back in any way.

"What do you mean, you gonna drop out?" Nonno asked, the sudden thickening of his Neapolitan accent the only evidence of his rising temper. "What you mean, college is no for you?"

Matthew swallowed thickly. "I only mean—maybe it isn't working out."

"No working out."

I winced. Nonno didn't yell. But when he repeated

things like that—things that he obviously thought were idiotic—it was a sign that trouble was brewing.

And my brother undoubtedly knew that.

"I just don't see the point." Matthew speared another piece of pasta onto his fork, then immediately shook it back onto the plate. "I'm not going to use any of these classes. Who cares about art history or the Napoleonic wars or any of the other dumb stuff they're making me learn?"

"*Dio*, no," Nonna murmured, crossing herself quickly, as if to prepare for the impending wrath of God. Or, at the very least, her husband.

With a nervous glance her way, Matthew continued. "I don't need a degree to get a job, Nonno. Writing papers and reading a bunch of textbooks isn't helping the family. I can do more here."

"Do more like what?" Nonno asked in a dangerously even voice.

"I don't know. Work in the shop, maybe. I can replace brake fluid and rebuild an engine or two. And God knows you need help in the office. Lea only helps with the books two nights a week, and that's only because you don't trust the boys alone with her. You wouldn't have to worry about that with me. We could expand, make Zola Auto into a franchise, you know?"

Out of the corner of my eyes, I caught Michael's glance at me when Matthew mentioned my name. I ignored it, too caught up with Matthew's proposals.

"And you think you're gonna get big money there? If the shop was gonna make us rich, we would be *rich*, no?" Nonno shook his head, clearly disgusted. "All this time. All this school. What do you think happens to boys like you *che* no go to school? Too many kids in the tiny apartment. Work themselves into nothing, if they lucky, or else they get into no good, I tell you! They do bad things, Matthew, they end up—"

Abruptly, Nonno cut off his own diatribe, though he wasn't able to keep from cutting his gaze directly at Michael. Our guest had also stopped eating and was watching the exchange along with the rest of us, though his fork still rested between his callused fingers.

"Like me," Michael finished softly, though with a rumble like one of the engines he worked on. "He means they end up like me." He blinked around the table as something clearly occurred to him. "That's why I'm here, isn't it? I'm someone you can help, but maybe also an example to your family. What could happen if they take the wrong path."

"No, Michael," I started to protest.

He continued like I hadn't even spoken, his voice almost meditative as he turned his water glass back and forth on the table, making a bit of light reflect onto the shiny wood top.

"It's all right. I don't mind being the example. Because that is what happened to me. I dropped out at fifteen. Ran off from the last group home six months later. Barely got my GED, and that was only because I was in prison with nothing better to do the last two years. Before that, I spent my time rolling with my boys, up to no good. And they never had my best interests at heart. Not like your grandparents have for you. I never had a family like that."

He took a sip of water. Matthew opened his mouth as if to argue. But before he could, Michael kept going.

"It wasn't 'if' I was going to get into trouble," he said after setting his glass back onto the table. "Just a matter of when. Now I'm paying for it. Struggling to make ends meet because one dumb move is going to follow me around the rest of my life. Meanwhile, the people I *thought* were my friends dropped me like a bad habit the second I went in." He shook his head. "I got nothing today but a minimum-wage job and a room above a garage, thanks to your grandpa here, and dinner that's not day-old pizza, thanks to his lovely wife. And I'm grateful because when I leave, I'll be right back where I started. I'll go to that break-room couch and stare up at the ceiling, thinking of how the hell I got there. And believe me when I say I won't wonder if a midnight joy ride was worth giving up my whole future—I can tell you right now it wasn't."

He took a bite of manicotti, chewed with relish, and swallowed before speaking again, seemingly unaware of the way my entire family was hanging on his every word.

"Take my word for it, *Matthew*—you don't want to go that route. Listen to the people who love and support you. Finish school. Get a job that doesn't pay by the hour. Set up house and build a family of your own, if that's what you want. But don't cut off your own feet before you even start the race. Do yourself at least that much. Do *them* at least that much. Do better than me."

Michael went back to quietly eating his pasta as if he hadn't spoken at all. His features were placid. The only sign he was affected was the slight flush rising over his cheekbones and the way his ears pinked at the tips.

It took at least three solid bites before anyone spoke again.

"Scarrone," Matthew said with a wide-eyed, shocked expression. "I, uh, wow. Honestly, man. I didn't even know you knew that many words."

One corner of Michael's mouth ticked upward. "Guess I was saving them up for you."

"That was a big speech," Joni remarked to Marie.

"Long too," Marie agreed.

"Hush," I told them. "Don't be rude."

"Did—did you want to add anything?" Matthew asked Nonno. Though his challenge was only half-hearted now. That defiant gaze now dropped back to his plate, where he pushed some ricotta around in a circle with his fork.

Nonno's focus, however, had transferred to Michael. He watched him with something like surprise. Surprise, but also respect.

He didn't look at very many people that way.

I was starting to understand why he had asked Michael to use his given name.

I was starting to understand a lot of things.

"No," Nonno said. "I think that's enough."

He nodded at Michael, who returned the gesture before dipping back to his meal, still acting like he had commented on the weather instead of my brother's future.

Immediately, the typical Zola racket rose again, as Matthew and Nonno began discussing Matthew's course load, Nonna helped Joni and Marie cut their manicotti, and Kate and Frankie debated the merits of Matthew's failed rebellion.

I stole glances at the man sitting next to me, who seemed content to fade into the background as easily as he had stolen the spotlight.

"Hey," I said, nudging his shoulder.

Michael's dark brows rose in challenge like he was expecting an argument.

"Pass the salad," I said, pointing to the bowl on the other side of him. "We haven't gotten it on this side."

He blinked, then obediently handed it to me.

His own plate, however, was bare of anything green.

I held it back out, holding the bowl so he could serve himself. "You should eat your vegetables. They're good for you."

He blinked at me—this time with a bit of humor. "I don't really like them."

"What are you, five? Even my baby sister eats her greens." I shoved the bowl at him. "Take some. They'll make you grow big and strong."

Michael hid a smile, but not before it caused a pair of dimples to make an appearance. "What, I ain't big enough for you?"

Something about that particular question made me shiver. It was meant as a joke, but it sounded like a dare. The kind that made my cheeks heat.

I glanced around to see if anyone else had overheard our little exchange, but my family was still too caught up in their own banter.

"*That*," I said to him, "remains to be seen."

Michael stifled a cough and slapped his chest.

"Eat," I pressed. "Don't offend the host."

That apparently motivated him, since he served

himself a bit of salad—greens dressed simply with olive oil and balsamic vinegar.

"All right," Michael said with a mild smirk as I took the bowl back and started to serve myself. "You win, contessa."

"Contessa?" I wondered.

That was a first.

The dimples returned, and this time, they stuck around.

"Sure," he said. "You're not a spoiled princess, but you're not a queen yet either. You're someone in the middle. A contessa."

I sucked in a breath. Coming from him, the nickname didn't sound exactly like teasing anymore. It sounded like something more mischievous. Something naughty.

I wasn't sure I liked it.

I also wasn't sure I didn't.

SEVEN

I DIDN'T ASK FOR IT, BUT I GOT IT ANYWAY

Michael

"I'm out of here," Tony called from the other side of the garage. "Scarrone, you're off the clock, you know that?"

I slid out from under the belly of the Town Car I was working on. The morning after I'd survived the Spanish Inquisition (aka Matthew Zola), Mattias had surprised me by offering weekend overtime to service a fleet he partially owned. Since then, I'd been up to my ears in oil changes, fluid replacement, and brake checks.

It was becoming clear to me that, despite his rant about money to Matthew, Mattias Zola had his fingers in a whole lot of car-related pies, and the shop in Belmont was just one of them. On their own, they didn't amount to much, but taken together, I was guessing they paid for that cozy house a few blocks from Arthur Avenue, the three younger kids' tuition at the parish school elementary school, and good meals for all of them every night of the week. He'd built a solid life for his family, and now he was letting me in on it.

I recognized it as the honor it was. But even so, I was dog fuckin' tired. Once Tony and I were clocked out, I trudged upstairs, ready for a shower, a beer, and bed, in that exact order.

Unfortunately, I wasn't getting any of them. Not when I opened the door to a room that was no more recognizable to me now than it was the first time I'd seen it.

To start, the place was clean. Gone were the grime on the walls, the dust bunnies in the corners, and the grease marks on the linoleum. Everything was sparkling and bright and smelled like lemons on a summer day.

The couch had also been made into a bed—pulled out, supplied with a mattress, and dressed with actual sheets, quilts, and pillows. The rest of the room had been equally transformed, with curtains, lamps, and even a lacy-looking tablecloth over the table in the corner.

"What the fuck?" I turned back around to make sure I hadn't wandered into another spare apartment.

Was there another set of stairs leading to another breakroom where another recent parolee was remaking his life?

"You're in the right place."

I whirled around to find Lea Zola standing at my stove, wearing a pair of jeans, purple high tops, and a tight white T-shirt that hugged every curve she had beneath a simple black apron. She was stirring something that smelled too fucking good in a big metal pot while another gurgled with boiling water.

"What are you doing here?" I demanded. "This is my apartment."

She snorted. "We've been over this, Michael. It's just a breakroom. But I'm working on it."

I gazed around, taking in the changes that had magically happened while I was at work. The walls weren't bare anymore, now holding a few pieces of framed art. Prints of things I vaguely remember seeing in school textbooks years ago. Sunflowers and waterlilies and a bowl of pears. A cross hung above the table, along with medieval-looking portraits of Saint Christopher and Saint Nicholas.

Oh, she thought she was witty. The original Santa Claus also happened to be the patron saint of thieves. Either Lea was informed about what I'd done, or she was making some assumptions I wasn't really a fan of.

Some of the cupboards were open, revealing a few shelves stacked with food. When she opened the fridge, that was stocked too. With enough to last me weeks.

Lea grabbed a package of spaghetti, ripped it open, and dumped it into the boiling water. I watched as if in a trance. What the fuck was going on?

"You made me dinner," I said, unable to keep the irritation out of my voice.

Lea stirred the pot. "Correct. You had, like, five helpings of manicotti last week. Obviously, you need real food in your stomach, not whatever crap you're picking up at the bodega. You know half the food they sell is expired, right? The owner replaces the stickers when he can."

I huffed. "I didn't ask you to do this for me. I can take care of myself."

"Good thing I didn't do it for you, then."

"Oh, you didn't?" I asked as I kicked off my boots and left them by the front door. "Is that why you're in this room stirring sauce instead of your own house?"

Lea snorted. It would have been kind of adorable if she wasn't such a damn know-it-all. "If I didn't do it, my grandmother would, whether you deserve it or not. But she has six kids and a husband to feed—she doesn't need to be worrying over you too. So this is for *her*, jackass, not you."

"Just like the blankets and the decorations are for your family too, not me?" I argued back, though I was basically transfixed as she scooped some spaghetti into a bowl and topped it with the sauce from the other pot.

"That's right," she said as she set the pasta on the table. "It will give them peace of mind, knowing you aren't wasting away up here. Now, eat."

I didn't want to follow her command any more than I wanted to sit down, but it smelled too damn good not to. I had all sorts of comebacks ready until I took a bite. Instead, I groaned. "Holy fuck, that is good."

Lea smiled as she joined me at the table. Her teeth were so white, but I didn't think that was the reason the whole room seemed to glow when she was in it.

"Thanks," she said. "My nonna taught me to cook."

"Well, she did a bang-up job, baby girl," I said through another mouthful of pasta. "This might be the best meal I've ever had."

Lea sat back, looking satisfied. "Don't get excited. Anyone in this neighborhood could make spaghetti."

"You don't sell yourself short." I glanced between the pot and her empty plate. "You gonna have some?"

She shook her head. "No, I gotta get home and get ready for a party. My friends are coming over at seven."

"What party is that?" I was barely listening, already halfway done with my plate and thinking about seconds. Probably thirds.

"You're not going? Matthew said you and Morris Carrera are friends."

I frowned while I chewed some more spaghetti. Christ, if I kept eating this family's food, I was going to gain fifty pounds. Not that I was going to stop. It was that damn good.

But it wasn't quite enough to distract me from the fact that she and her brother had been talking about me. And probably talking about my past. "That was a long time ago. I don't really party anymore."

Understatement of the year.

"Isn't that what you're supposed to be doing at twenty-one?" Lea wondered.

"Getting drunk with high school students?" I asked, enjoying the way it made her cheeks redden. "Nah, I'll pass."

"Morris graduated with you," she pointed out. "And I'm eighteen. This party is adults-only."

I chuckled. "Keep telling yourself that, contessa."

The bright smile on her pretty face told me I'd injected some hope into the situation by teasing her. If I hadn't known it before, I did now—my boss's grand-daughter had a little crush. Too bad I was the exact wrong person for her to want.

"Morris graduated after I dropped out," I said as I built another bite. "I couldn't stay."

"Why, because you had so many more important things to do?"

I snorted. "Yeah. Like going to jail. Big fuckin' loser over here, remember?"

That shut her up. In fact, she looked downright mad. For a moment, I thought she might actually leave, but as I focused on my food and *not* on her reddened cheeks, she said the one thing I was not expecting.

"Sorry. That was a shitty thing to say."

I put down my fork. "Yeah, it was. But so was throwing my record in your face."

"I was an idiot. I'm sorry. I'll—I'll just go."

Quickly, Lea got up and started for the door, face pinked with embarrassment. The effect was immediate. Almost like I was watching myself do it, I was out of my chair, crossing the room, and had my hand slapped on the door to keep her from leaving.

"It's fine," I said over her shoulder. "Don't go. Stay. Have dinner with me."

It sounded like a lot more of an invitation than I intended. People our age didn't go out to dinner. We partied. We hung out. We talked on the phone and flirted on doorsteps. We didn't sit down like regular-ass adults and treat girls we barely knew, but really fuckin' liked, to steak or pasta.

But right then, with her flowery scent floating up from her hair and the warmth of her compact body trapped between me and the door, the idea of taking Lea Zola out on the town, where everyone could see her sitting with me, dressed up for me, eating the dinner I bought her...

Yeah, that sounded like the best idea in the world.

Unfortunately, all I could offer was the dinner *she* made.

Well, at least we could share.

"I'm sorry," she said for the third time as she turned.

I was getting really tired of hearing her say that.

I tipped her chin up, forcing her to focus those emerald beauties up at me. "It's fine. Besides, you're right."

That adorable, eleven-shaped divot appeared between her brows. "Right about what?"

I shrugged. "I am a no-good piece of shit."

"I never said—"

"You meant it," I said. "And it's true. That's why I landed at Rikers. Things like that don't happen to good people. People like your brother. People like you."

She chewed on that for a second. I *hated* that she even had to think it over.

I returned to the table, satisfied when she moved back to the kitchenette, made herself a small bowl of pasta, and took the other folding chair at the table.

"Well, that's some bullshit," Lea said stoutly as she twisted some spaghetti with her fork.

I swallowed a mouthful of my own and looked up. "Say what?"

She straightened up as far as she could. She wasn't a big person—maybe five foot four and change—but somehow, she managed to occupy a lot of space when she wanted to. She practically demanded attention before she even spoke.

"I said," she repeated, as she tucked a lock of hair behind one ear, "that's bullshit."

She took a large bite, as if repeating the statement a third time.

"What's bullshit?"

"The idea that people are bad or good. That what happened to you is all you are, and that's all you'll ever be. It's bullshit." She took another bite, chewed and swallowed, then continued. "'Let the one among you who is without sin be the first to throw a stone' and all that."

I smirked. "Easy to say when you're Jesus."

She smiled. It lit up her whole face—of course, all a sinner like me had to do was mention Jesus to make her smile. Fuck, I was *all* wrong for her.

"I knew you knew your Bible," she said, going back to her food. "Good people don't forget the Good Book, Michael."

I chuckled as I continued eating. "That's not morals; it's five years of catechism, Tess. And I got kicked out before confirmation."

Her brow furrowed adorably. "Tess?"

I grinned. "Tess for contessa. Or would you prefer Your Majesty?"

For that, I received an eye roll. Then she looked thoughtful. "Then why did Father Deflorio want to help you? He wouldn't go out of his way for a lost cause."

I shrugged. "I'm the stain on his spotless record. It drives him nuts that I'm the only kid he ever had to kick out of catechism classes for bad behavior. Makes him a hypocrite."

"But clearly, you know your Scripture," she replied, pointing at me with a bit of noodle on her fork.

"Everyone knows the Book of John."

"Not enough to cite it."

I opened my mouth to argue. But she had me there.

"You're like a wolf cub, see," she went on after a few more minutes. "And you know, they can go either way."

"Oh, yeah? What do you know about wolves in the city?"

"I know one when I see one. Just like I know some wolves run with the pack. But others, sometimes they have to be on their own. Sometimes, they become lone wolves. And once that happens, they're done for." Lea tipped her head. "But you're not a lone wolf yet, Michael Scarrone. You came to stay in a den. You let me in. There's hope for you yet."

Suddenly, my mouth was very dry. I grabbed my water glass and chugged the entire thing, if only to avoid her searching expression. What the fuck did she want me to do? To admit she was right? To say that deep down, I wanted a place, a home, a family like hers? That if, by some miracle, Lea Zola would be content to cook for me and boss me around and make a place like this for me, I'd consider myself the luckiest man alive?

Well, if that's what she wanted, she could wait all fuckin' night. I wasn't going to waste my time on fantasies that were less likely to be real than Santa Claus himself. The dude on my wall was more likely than me to achieve the American dream.

"So what did you do?" she asked, without a fucking iota of shame, as I shoved another bit of pasta into my mouth. "Why did they put you away?"

I practically choked. She watched, clearly amused,

while I pounded my chest and somehow managed to swallow.

"I—did you really ask me that again?" I croaked. "You put the patron saint of *thieves* on my wall, for Christ's sake."

Lea shrugged. "Lucky guess, and it was only twenty-five cents at the Salvation Army. Listen, I figure my nonno already knows, but I want to hear it from you. He wouldn't let you stay here if you were a rapist or a murderer or something like that, so I'm not worried that it's really bad. You can let him tell me, or you can tell me yourself. I'll find out either way."

She had some nerve; I had to give her that. She didn't look away. Not once. Those green eyes stared right at me, waiting, waiting for me to answer.

Come out with it, they said.

Fuck it. I might as well.

"I stole a car," I said.

"What kind?"

I scowled. "A 1994 Honda Civic."

"EX? LX?"

I narrowed my eyes. "You want to know the trim of the car I stole?"

She shrugged, like she'd asked about the weather. "It would affect the resale value. Don't forget, I basically grew up in an auto shop. Call me curious."

I sighed around another bite of pasta while she watched me chew, waiting not-so-patiently for my answer. "It was a three-door hatchback, five-speed coupe DX, with a hundred and thirty-five thousand miles and a faulty transmission."

I got up without waiting for her response.

Honestly, I didn't want to see the disappointment on her face. People want to believe that if you're going to go to prison for something like grand larceny, the price of the thing you stole is comparable to the price you pay for stealing it. Then they find out you lost everything for the most common car in America. Suddenly, you're not only dangerous—you're also stupid.

Letting the ceramic clink a little too hard, I stacked her bowl on top of mine, then carried them to the sink and started doing dishes.

It was no good, though. Less than a minute later, Lea popped up next to me and started putting away the leftover food in Tupperware that apparently now filled the second drawer under the counter. She'd made enough pasta for an army. I'd be eating that delicious sauce for a week.

"A ninety-four Civic worth *maybe* three grand seems like a crappy car to risk your life for," she said.

I grunted. Couldn't argue there.

"So?" she asked.

"So, what?"

"So, why'd you do it?"

"Because I felt like it," I snapped, splashing my shirt with soapy water in the process. "I was bored one day, and I decided to take a joy ride. Saw the car, wanted the car, took the car. Simple as that."

She didn't say anything. In fact, she stopped moving altogether, abandoning the leftovers to lean against the counter and stare at me with her arms crossed.

"What?" I asked after I couldn't fuckin' take it anymore.

"What, yourself? Don't play games with me, Michael."

"What games?" I bit out, going hard at a nonexistent stain on her perfectly clean bowl. "It's the truth, plain and simple."

"I don't believe you."

"Well, you should."

"And why exactly is that?"

"Because I'm no fuckin' good!" I exploded as I tossed the bowl onto the dish rack with a clatter and threw the scrubber into the water. More of it splashed on my shirt. I barely noticed. "The sooner you get that through your pretty little head, the better. I do bad things, Lea. I steal cars. I sleep around. I fuck up. That's all there is to it. All there is to *me*."

Lea was quiet for another long minute. Eventually, I went back to cleaning, but there wasn't much more to do. Two glasses. Two bowls. A few forks. That was all. The sum total of this borrowed kitchenette. This borrowed life.

My hand was practically shaking when I finally turned off the water. Then Lea finally spoke.

"You're a liar," she said in a husky voice that barely quavered so slightly that no one else would have noticed.

But I did. I had a feeling I would always notice things like that about Lea Zola.

"What have I been telling you?" I asked. "You don't know me for shit, baby girl."

"I know you enough," she shot back, even as she pushed herself off the counter.

She had that look about her. The look of a woman

who was on her way out, even before she made the move.

Something in my chest tightened as I watched her march around the kitchenette, gathering a few things she'd brought from her house, packing them into the shopping bag, then finally slinging on her coat before she headed for the door.

It was only after she twisted the knob that she stopped to face me again.

"Maybe you're right. Maybe I don't really know you, Michael Scarrone," she said quietly. "But God does. And he hates a liar too."

"Yeah, well, God left me out of his plans years ago," I said bitterly. "That's how I ended up here. In case you forgot."

She shook her head stubbornly, causing her hoop earrings to sway from side to side. "I don't think so. I think you're here because of those plans. And one way or another, we're going to figure them out." She opened the door, then paused once more. "The party's in Port Morris, near Mill Brook Houses. In case you want to start fresh there, too."

"Fuck the party," I bit out. "And fuck this dinner, too. It was good, but I don't need any more of your handouts, contessa. I can take care of myself."

Even as I spoke, I knew I was confirming everything she'd thought of me. That I was a wolf, so desperate not to be trapped again that I'd bite everyone, even chew off my own foot, to avoid it.

Lea, however, didn't bite back. Not this time.

"At least you have some fight in you," she said as she stepped out of the room. "Good thing, too. My nonno wouldn't hire a pussy." She sniffed. "Next time I'll bring a salad. I already know you don't eat enough vegetables."

And before I could answer, she left.

But not before two words rang in my ear a few seconds too late.

Mill Brook.

One of the most notorious housing projects in the Bronx. Home to gangbangers, dealers, vagrants, and who knew how many junkies with eyes for pretty young women.

Lea Zola, the innocent girl who had apparently decided to save my godforsaken soul, was entering a den of sin.

A party I absolutely did not want to attend.

And yet, deep down, I already knew I was going. When it came to her, I was starting to think I didn't really ever have a choice. Maybe I didn't want one either.

EIGHT

LITTLE PINK DRESS, WHOLE LOTTA TROUBLE

Lea

"I cannot believe I let you talk me into this dress, Ang."

For the tenth time since getting off the bus, I tugged the hem of the magenta pink dress—if you could even call it that—down so it would actually cover my butt. I wouldn't have ever called myself a prude (even if my friends would), but this dress was testing my limits.

"Will you shut up about the freaking dress, Le?" Angie replied while Linda rolled her eyes. "You talked yourself into it. You said yourself you wanted to look like sex on wheels. I just provided the gas."

I'd never been much of a partier, had never even tried to sneak into the clubs downtown like my friends sometimes did. There was too much to do at home. When Angie had been invited when we were all walking out of sixth period Calculus together, I had originally passed, like I normally did.

But the feeling that everyone—my friends, my family, even my little sisters—was leaving me behind kept bugging me through the week, like a cold I couldn't shake. And the second Michael Scarrone looked at me that way—like I was a priceless heirloom, untouched and unspoiled, a perfect little virgin he couldn't even *think* of messing up—my mind changed completely.

I'd left the garage and called Angie to let her know I was coming over. She and Linda had jumped at the opportunity to dress me up in something miles from the parade of jeans and T-shirts I typically wore. Now, I was paying the price while I followed my friends under an actual freeway, hoping we wouldn't get murdered on our way to one of Morris Carrera's legendary underground parties.

"I might look hot, but I am fuh-reezing," I told her. "How many more blocks do we have? This neighborhood is freaking me out."

We'd been walking since getting off the bus. Mott Haven wasn't exactly the Ritz, but on the other side of the 278 was Port Morris, a district made up mostly of warehouses. For the last few blocks, we'd ignored a few harmless vagrants, but mostly, we were on the lookout for people who were waiting for idiots like us to stumble in their paths.

Everyone who grows up in New York knows one thing: a silent block is always more dangerous than a lively one. It's the quiet places that are the scariest. And this place was completely dead.

"I think it's another block this way," Angie said.

"You didn't print out the directions?" Linda demanded.

"Bish, I don't have a printer. And I was too busy making over this one to run down to the library, you know?"

We all chuckled.

"You're gonna thank me when we get to the party and every guy is drooling over you," Angie added, looking over me again like she was appraising her work.

"Lord knows enough of them wanted it on the bus," I returned. "Why do they all think calling 'hey ma' is going to turn me on?"

"Or whistling from across the street?" Angie added.

"It's like dogs needing to piss on things," Linda replied as we turned around yet another seemingly abandoned corner. "They can't help it. It's the first step to marking their territory."

"Speaking of dogs, is your brother going to be here tonight?" Angie wondered slyly.

I sent her a narrow-eyed look. Angie had been trying for years to catch Matthew's eye, to no avail.

"No. He has a test. And you have got to stop barking up that tree, Ange. Sherry Alvarez won't be letting him go any time soon."

It was no secret that I didn't like my brother's girl-friend, but he'd made it clear that he didn't care about my opinion or anyone else's in the family long ago.

"Ugh, gross. She is such a skank!" Angie whined. "Why would he want that when he could have big-mouthed perfection right here?"

"She is pretty, though," Linda remarked, always the fair one. "I like what she did to her hair."

"Pretty is as pretty does," I said.

"You sound like my mom, Le," Angie joked.

A thump of bass reverberated through the air. Followed by another. And another.

We all swung toward it like dogs at a whistle.

"That has to be it," Angie said.

It was.

The building was huge and clearly abandoned, but the graffiti-covered door was wide open, and the music pounded like a heartbeat into the night. As we got closer, I could feel the vibration of the bass from my chest down to my toes.

Well, at least they didn't have frostbite in these nearly naked sandals.

"Ten bucks each," said the doorman, who I recognized as one of the linemen on the Belmont Prep football team.

"Come on, John. You can let us in, can't you?" Angie whined, sticking out her chest as she spoke.

John shook his head. I had a feeling those weren't the first ta-tas shaken at him this evening. "Nah. Ten bucks a pop, Ange."

It was worth a try.

Inside, the building was packed, and the air was heavy with sweat and cheap booze. At least two hundred people were dancing and grinding up on each other in time to the music pouring from speakers set up all around the periphery, all controlled by a DJ spinning vinyl on a pair of turntables set up on a rickety stage. To the sides of the makeshift booth, a few kids, one or two of which I recognized from school, were mouthing lyrics to themselves, clearly getting ready for the inevitable battle that always took place at parties like these.

Hands were roving, mouths puckering, bodies heaving. Sex was in the air, thick and overt. This definitely wasn't a place for wallflowers.

I considered turning around. I could still go back to my typical night. Help Nonna with the girls, do a little extra studying, and maybe pop in a movie with Kate. It wasn't too late. Almost no one had seen me yet, and therefore no one would laugh either if I cut and run with my tail between my legs.

But then I thought of Michael and the way he'd snapped at me earlier. And I decided that something out of character, something *un*safe, was exactly what I should be doing on a Friday night of my last year in high school. Preferably as soon as possible.

"Let's get a drink," Linda shouted over the music, gesturing toward a line of people waiting for red Solo cups. There were several stands like it set up throughout the party, each manned by two people—one to serve drinks, one to collect the money.

We pushed our way through the crowd, and I couldn't help but feel multiple pairs of eyes looking my way. I'd wanted this, hadn't I? For once, I wasn't the practical older sister, Nonna's good girl, straight-A student, blah, blah, blah. Right now, I was the object of desire. It was exactly what I wanted.

That was when I finally smiled.

We waited in line until we found Robbie Caldera— one of my middle school classmates—poured a neon-orange liquid into the red Solo cups, while his buddy collected three dollars to put into a Ziploc bag.

"Yo, Lea fuckin' Zola!" Robbie crowed when he caught sight of me, his eyes the size of stoplights. "Damn, that is some dress, there, mami. You look stupid hot!"

"Thanks," I said, preening a little. "What's in the cooler?"

Robbie offered a sly smile. "Jungle juice. It's a mystery. Little of this, little of that, you know. You want?"

I shrugged. What the hell? I was already in Rome. I might as well do as they did.

We handed over the cash, and Robbie eagerly handed over the drinks.

"Bottoms up, babies," Angie called out, and together, my friends and I downed our first lethal cup.

THIRTY MINUTES LATER, I was practically on the floor. It's not like I'd never drank before. My grandparents never shied from letting us kids taste a bit of wine here and there with dinner. But for the most part, I avoided alcohol, too conscious of the fact that it had cost me both of my parents.

For the first time, I finally understood why people liked it so much. The vodka—or whatever the hell was in this so-called Jungle Juice—had gone straight to my head. I was feeling damn good.

"I'm gonna go dance," I called to my friends, leaning over the table to shout in their ears.

Linda looked up from where she had been flirting a little too much with Robbie. "Wait for us."

But I was already heading toward the dance floor in front of the DJ booth. Dancing was one of those things I'd mostly done alone. Sure, Kate and I had done the requisite "choreography" to Janet Jackson and Mary J. Blige when we were kids. But these days, I didn't really let loose in a house where everyone loved to tease and where I had to maintain at least some authority.

Right now, though, I didn't care what anyone thought of me. My body felt loose, my limbs light, as I moved my hips to the latest dancehall beat. I felt no shame in shaking my ass like those girls on MTV I'd always made fun of. For once, *I* could be like those video girls.

So this was why people liked to party. For the first time, I really got it.

The opening piano bars of "Still Dre" sounded through the warehouse, and the crowd went nuts.

"Hey, ma, you wanna dance?"

A pair of hands landed on my hips, and I strained my neck to see their owner. A guy who was maybe twenty licked his lips as he openly ogled my magenta-clad body. My lips felt like rubber as I let him draw me close enough to feel his cock—at least I thought that's what it was—harden against my hip. Close enough to know he wanted a lot more than a quick grind.

How did people do this when they had barely met?

A few couples away, I caught sight of Angie grinding with another guy and giving me the thumbs-up over his shoulder. She approved of the one who'd found me. I should have liked this. I should have wanted to continue.

But the boy's breath reeked of stale alcohol, even

through a breath mint. And close up, the pores on his nose were really clogged. And some of the hairs on his face were ingrown, causing an pimples around his chin.

I wrinkled my nose in distaste and stepped away. "Thanks, I'm good."

The kid looked genuinely shocked as he grabbed for my hand. "The fuck you mean? You chose me, rubbing your booty practically in my face."

"I let you grab my hip, not my pussy, jackass," I snapped, yanking my hand out of his.

I'd raised my voice loud enough to be heard even above Dr. Dre and Snoop. Moments like these were always a little dangerous, even in my limited experience. Nine times out of ten, pushy men like this one backed off like they were supposed to. No one wanted a crazy bitch yelling at them in front of their friends.

But sometimes, they came right back at you. Sometimes, they found you elsewhere. That was a whole other thing I'd never had the pleasure of experiencing.

But it was a risk a girl had to take for a bit of respect in places like these.

Luckily, this risk paid off.

Mr. Handsy backed away with a snarl, muttering unintelligible insults under his breath before he disappeared into the crowd.

Determined not to lose my chill, I continued to dance.

"Girl." Angie appeared beside me, Linda in tow. "What is up? Which one you want, Le? Take your pick. It's a buffet in here."

"I like the one over there in the orange shirt," Linda

remarked. "Isn't that Victor Jenkins's older brother? He's been staring at Lea all night."

I turned at the mention of my ex-boyfriend, if you could call him that. The one who had christened me Cherry Popper. Frigid. If he could see me now… "I— no. No…that's actually…oh my God, that's Victor."

As if he'd been summoned like a demon simply by saying his name.

He was a little older but a whole lot more grown-up. Still tall, of course. Well over six feet, with dark, wavy hair and sharp eyes, plus a well-groomed goatee to match his immaculate fade. His smile was always crooked, as if he were permanently amused. I hadn't seen him since he'd graduated from Belmont Prep. Two years that had transformed a skinny basketball star into an outright man.

Who was now looking at me.

And now, crossing the room.

And now, dodging dancers until he was standing. Right. Here.

"'Sup, Lea," he said, leaning down to kiss my cheek. "Long time no see."

"I—you look—" I said out of the corner of my mouth as his hands landed on my hips.

Something gleamed in Victor's eyes. "Thanks, babe. You look good too."

I exhaled. I felt like I couldn't move. "Don't."

A smirk played over those full lips that I had once seriously craved. "Don't what, Lea? You want me to let go?" Victor massaged my hips, moving lower with each pass. "Or maybe you want me to stop talking?" His eyes practically undressed me. "This dress…damn, girl. Why didn't you wear stuff like this when we were together?"

"Because you didn't fuckin' deserve it," Angie remarked, despite the fact that it was *her* dress I was wearing.

I swallowed, wondering why the hell my body didn't seem to want to follow my brain. Why my mouth had stopped working.

It's called alcohol, you idiot. And you'd know this if you got out more.

I knew what he wanted. Knew what I wanted. But not with him. Not after what he'd done.

"Asshole," I heard Angie mutter to Linda.

I was drunk, but it was enough to wake me up. I stepped out of Victor's grasp and rejoined my friends.

"It was nice to see you," I told him.

"Come on, babe, let's dance a little," Victor called. "Get to know each other a little more. Or are you still the Cherry Popper."

"Fuck off," Linda spat. "Don't nobody want *your* two-timing bullshit, Victor."

I didn't stop to see his reaction. I'd already turned on my heel and made for the Jungle Juice dispenser like it was an orange beacon calling me to safety.

"Lea," Angie called as my friends chased after me. "Le! Be careful. That shit is potent."

"Good," I said before tossing back another plastic cupful, and then holding it out to Robbie for more. "That's what I'm hoping for."

"Lea, maybe you wanna wait…" Robbie glanced nervously back and forth between me and my friends. Angie seemed to intimidate him.

"I already gave you an extra ten to keep it coming, Robbie," I snapped as I shoved my cup at him. "Fill it up."

After the third on, I was starting to feel like Alice falling down the rabbit hole. Everything was spinning. There was nothing to hold on to, so I might as well dive in all the way.

"What are you trying to do?" Linda asked. "Get drunk and get laid?"

"Maybe," I said as I caught Victor watching me, a sneer on his face while he chatted with another girl. They both start laughing with his friends. I turned away. "Maybe he's right. Maybe I should get it over with."

"Lea, come on," Linda replied. "Be reasonable. This is you we're talking about."

"I am being reasonable," I half-slurred. "I'm done being the last lamest virgin in Belmont who can't even string two sentences together when her lame ex-boyfriend licks his lips. Even my little sister beat me to the punch. It's *time*."

The pitying expressions on my friends' faces didn't help matters. It was plain they both agreed with me.

"So, that's it," I proclaimed. "I'm thinking, let's throw caution to the wind. Next new hottie I see who doesn't need Proactiv and who didn't already break my heart gets to pop this cherry. What do you think?"

Robbie Caldera's jaw about hit the floor before he scurried away, probably the share the news. Angie and Linda both exploded in giggles, but they didn't seem to be looking at the absent Jungle Juice monitor.

I frowned at them. "What?"

Okay, I was talking big, but I figured they'd be into it after the way they'd been pestering me all evening.

"Le," said Angie as she pointed over my shoulder. "Girl, I think you got your wish."

"Lea?"

The sound of my name in that familiar deep timbre set every hair on the back of my neck standing straight up.

"Is it…?" I mouthed to Angie, who laughed harder.

I looked around. And almost died right there.

At not quite six feet, he didn't tower over anyone, but he still managed to look like he could by the way his plain white T-shirt clung to his broad, squared shoulders. The material was practically indecent, thin enough that I could see tattooed shadows swirling up his biceps and under the cotton.

His dark hair was mussed, like he hadn't taken the time to do it. But it only added to the devil-may-care appeal in everything but his eyes—those dark, mournful, earnest eyes—as they traveled over the crowd, taking everything in.

Then they landed back on me. And did not move.

Even with the thumping bass and the noise of all these people packed into the warehouse, the party seemed to quiet as people stopped their conversations to take note of the most notable guest in their midst.

Michael Scarrone had arrived at the party.

And he'd heard everything I'd just said.

NINE

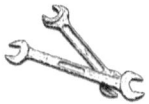

BUSTING UP THE CONQUISTADORS

Michael

I regretted going to Carrera's party before I even set foot in Port Morris. How many underground joints like this had I been to over the years? This was nothing more than another abandoned warehouse. Another mass of people. Another "legendary" get-together that was guaranteed to be broken up at three in the morning and cost at least one kid the rest of his life, thanks to the "War on Drugs" and Stop and Frisk.

There's a reason people call it the Boogie Down. People in the Bronx have always liked to party.

That isn't always a good thing.

Maybe it was still one of the poorest neighborhoods in the city, but everyone could smell the sea change when big companies were coming in and buying up lots for pennies. Developers would follow. High-rises were on the horizon. Yeah, the South Bronx was changing, like everywhere else in New York. But it was a long way from safe—maybe even less so for the people who had lived here the longest.

People like Lea Zola.

Who was the reason I found myself slapping hands with some of my old crew and greeting others with a nod or a "what's up?" while searching the crowd. I found her standing with her girls around a drinks table, tipping back Carrera's notorious Jungle Juice, while Robbie Caldera, wearing an expression a shark might while circling its prey, poured for them again and again.

And then she opened her mouth and shouted something straight out of every motherfucker in the party's wet dream: Next man she meets gets to hit that...for the first time.

Lea Zola just invited a warehouse full of conquistadors to invade her new world.

And I thought my fuckin' heart was gonna stop.

"I think you got your wish," said one of Lea's friends as I charged toward them like a bull.

Lea's big green eyes grew even bigger when she caught sight of me. Her perfect mouth was shiny with gloss and leftovers from her drink. She wore a tiny pink dress that was glued to her curves. I could see practically everything through the thin material—the outline of her navel, the curve of her hip, the exact shapes of her nipples.

Jesus *Christ.*

She was probably the most innocent thing in the room, but between the dress, the Barbie-looking heels, and the sleek black hair falling down her back, she was the perfect picture of sin. It was a hell of a contradiction and stopped my brain completely. It also hadn't escaped me that every dude in the room was now looking at her like a piece of very juicy meat. Something they would love to…pound.

Fucking *fuck*.

Her entire mood shifted as I approached—it was in the tilt of her hip and slight arch of her back. A subtle invitation, but it was there. And it disappeared the moment I spoke.

"What the *fuck* are you doing here?" I demanded.

Lea's luscious mouth dropped open. "*What* did you say?"

"Damn," her friend with the mini twists said. "Ange, did you hear that?"

"Jealous, much?" the other with shoulder-length blond hair replied.

I ignored them both as I grabbed Lea's hand and started towing her away with me.

To where? I couldn't have told you. It was instinct. All I knew was that every cell in my body was screaming at me to get her away. Away from prying eyes. Away from wandering hands. Away from anyone and everyone who saw only a piece of ass when I saw so much more.

Not for me.

Never for me.

But sure as shit not for any of them.

"What are you doing?" Lea cried. "Oh my God, Michael, what are you so freaking *mad* about?"

She wrenched her hand out of mine before I'd made it ten feet through the crowd. I scowled and grabbed it again, holding tighter when she tried to pull away and smack my shoulder.

"Fuckin' *stop*," I snapped.

"*You* stop," she retorted as she twisted her body in vain. "I don't know what you think you're doing, but you're causing a scene!"

"*I'm* causing a scene?" I turned then, holding fast to one spot. The people around us were smart enough to step out of punching distance. Though they were happy to watch, the fuckin' voyeurs. "You're the one who came to a party in a goddamn handkerchief. Does your nonno know you left the house looking like that?"

"Fuck. *Off!*" Lea cut back. "I am an adult in case you hadn't noticed. I can wear whatever the fuck I want."

I honestly think she would have bitten me if she could have. She did not, however, answer my question, which led me to believe that no, Mattias Zola had no clue his beautiful granddaughter was out here fueling the spank bank of every man here and probably a bunch more on her way.

She twisted her hand free, only for me to catch it again. This time, I hauled her to me and wrapped my arm around her shoulder.

"Who the fuck do you think you are?" Lea seethed, her nails digging into my arm as she tried to shove it off. "You can take this caveman shit and shove it up your ass, Scarrone!"

"Try that again, and I'll throw you over my shoulder and show you a caveman," I growled into her ear.

"Bite me."

"Baby girl, do not fuckin' tempt me."

If only she knew. She smelled so sweet, like that

godforsaken mix of at least five types of liquor overlaid with the floral scent of her hair.

I shouldn't have liked any of it, but I was hard as a rock.

Hard and furious. A toxic combination.

"You need somethin'?" I growled at a particularly hungry-eyed kid I barely recognized as Roland Nguyen, the dry-cleaner's kid. Over his shoulder, I noted her friends watching wryly, like they knew this was good for her, even if they weren't sure she would like it.

He shied immediately. "What up, Mike? Nothin', man, just—she's—"

"She's none of your fuckin' business," I snapped as I carted Lea toward the only other opening in the place besides the entrance.

"Cool, cool!" Roland called behind me. "I didn't know she's yours, man. I'll let everyone know!"

I didn't bother to correct him.

"What did he mean 'she's yours'?" Lea wondered. "I'm not yours. I'm not anyone's!"

I ignored her as I brought her out to a makeshift balcony. Four other people were already out there, enjoying a smoke while they looked across the East River toward...of course. Rikers fuckin' Island.

Well, it was a good reminder of what I didn't want to be anymore.

"Out," I ordered the people eyeing us through a cloud of cigarette smoke.

"Scarrone!" answered one of them. "What the fuck, man, I heard you—"

"I need a minute," I said to whoever had said my

name. Honestly, right now, I didn't fucking care. I was too mad.

Quickly, they cleared out. For once, I was glad I had a reputation. It made moments like these easier. Nothing clears a room like a bad fuckin' temper.

"What the hell, Michael?" Lea demanded once I finally let her go. "You *dragged* me out here for no reason! That was so embarrassing!"

"*That* was embarrassing?" I exploded. "Sweetheart, you just announced to half the fuckin' Bronx that you're willing to give your virginity to the next dude in line."

"Oh, please. That was obviously a joke."

"Yeah? Tell them that." I gestured toward the party.

Hungry gazes were still flickering her way from the other side of the wide-open door. The singsong melody of the latest underground Aventura song danced its way toward us, much to the delight of the party. I rolled my eyes. Another song about a dude obsessed with a woman he can't have. Fitting.

Lea glared at me but didn't lash out again. Instead, she wrapped her arms around her slim body. Her nipples had perked up even more in the winter chill, and the rest of her bare skin rippled with goose bumps.

"Y-you're imp-possible," she chattered.

"Here," I said, holding out the black wool jacket I'd stripped off as soon as I'd entered the party. "Put this on because you're not going back in there."

"I didn't ask for this," she said, though she allowed me jacket around her shoulders. "Get *off* me!"

"I'm off, I'm off, contessa." I held up my hands as I took a step backward. "God, you're even bossier when you're wasted."

I expected her to bolt, but to my surprise, she didn't. Instead, she stood there glaring at me, the most beautiful little minx I'd ever seen. Regal, even when she was toasted.

"You dressed up again," she said a few moments later.

I looked down at my clothes. It was the same thing I wore to her grandparents' house, except I'd exchanged a white T-shirt for the button-down. The jacket wasn't much—Father Deflor had let me raid it from the church's Lost and Found. The clothes weren't exactly stylish, but they were clean. Apparently I had set the bar for "nice" pretty damn low.

"I guess," I said. "It's my only coat. And I needed to be warm for the walk."

She balked. "You *walked* here from Belmont? That would take like an hour and a half."

I ground my teeth, unwilling to admit that I wasn't about to waste the last forty dollars I had on subway fare or a cab when I had two perfectly good legs. "Yeah."

What else was I supposed to say? That I wasn't going to come at all? That I was fully planning to eat more of the dinner she'd cooked, then fall asleep flipping through one of the decade-old magazines Mattias kept in his office for waiting customers? But that once I'd flopped onto the bed *she* had made up for me, I'd stared at the ceiling until I couldn't fuckin' take it no more and then walked the hour and thirty-three minutes through Crotona Park, down Union Avenue, and under the freeway, all the while imagining how Lea might have been picked up at any corner, until I'd walked into this party and seen every dude in here imagining how he might do just that.

It was my worst nightmare come to life.

"What are *you* doing at a place like this, Lea?" I asked abruptly.

Her scowl returned. "What, a nice girl like me?" she asked bitterly, as she clutched my jacket tighter. "I told you I was coming."

"Girl like you deserves to be wined and dined. Not humped in the projects on some joker's mattress."

She looked back at the building, then at me. "This isn't the projects."

"Next thing to it. Carrera lives in Mill Brook now, you know. Half the party probably lives in his building."

"So, if they live in a housing project, they're not good enough for me?"

"Don't be fuckin' naive, Lea."

She recoiled at my tone. "There's the wolf again."

I took a deep breath. I was snapping like a feral animal. Wrong idea, especially when I wanted to protect her, even if I had no business trying.

"You know what goes on here," I tried again, this time more carefully. "You know what's going on here *right now*. Half the people in this party are either high or looking to score. There's gonna be more than one fight breaking out before the night is over. Not to mention plenty of dudes looking to get you so wasted, you pass out in their arms, and they can take you home and do whatever they want. You're better than them, Lea. You deserve better than this."

She was quiet for a long time, but those green eyes sparked like firecrackers. It was everything I could do not to look away—but I wouldn't stand down. Not about this.

She, however, was not about to let me off the hook, either.

"I'm sorry about, ah, dragging you out here," I said finally. I had to give her something. "I could have talked to you in there, I guess."

"And?"

I swallowed, frowned, and sighed. In that order. "And…I'm sorry for yelling at you. And for insulting your dress. You, um, you actually look nice tonight. Really fuckin' nice. Too nice—shit."

What the hell was happening? I went from being a caveman to a wolf to a bumbling fuckin' idiot. And yet, I found I meant it. Lea had obviously been feeling herself in there, and she looked all the better for it. It wasn't her fault that part of my brain wanted to cover her up so I was the only man who had the pleasure of seeing her like this. That wasn't fair to her. Or anyone else.

When I managed to look back at her, the anger on her face had all but evaporated. She looked unsure. But also, maybe a little curious.

"I think," she said carefully. "That you have the wrong idea about me."

"And what idea is that?" I asked as I watched her cross the balcony to stand next to me.

This was dangerous. This close, I could smell those sweet flowers again. Feel her body breathing next to mine in the dark. See, all too clearly, the way her skin glistened under that dress—*fuck*.

"That I need money to be happy," she said.

"Restaurants or cars or shit like that. I'm still in freaking high school, Michael. I share a room with my sister. I'm not fancy."

I swallowed. "Aren't you?" Compared to my life, hers was the lap of luxury.

Out here, in only the ambient light of the party, the end of her nose red with the cold, she looked like a goddamn queen in her dress and tiny silver shoes, my coat thrown over her shoulders like a cape.

No, not a queen. A contessa.

My contessa.

The thought entered my head before I could stop it. All I knew was that she deserved the fucking moon if she could find a man to give it to her. And I would have sawed off my arm to be that man.

"I live as crowded as everyone else we know," she argued. "Everyone in my family shares a room except Mattie, and he lives in an unfinished attic, like Cinderella. We hand down every piece of clothing we own. We might drink wine sometimes, but it's the cheapest we can find. But we don't care. Like you said to my brother—it's the people in our lives who matter more than anything else."

"I—yeah, I guess," I said as she stepped close enough that if I looked down, I'd see her bare toes framed between my big, clumsy feet.

Instead, I leaned against the railing, trying to give her the out. Trying to let her get away, before I snatched her up for myself.

"I think you have a secret," she told me as her fingers walked up my shirt.

"Oh, yeah?" My voice was hoarse, like I'd just been shouting.

"Yeah." Her mouth was barely a few inches from mine, her heels granting a bit more height. "I think you're actually a good person, deep down."

I shook my head, though she moved even closer. "Nah. I'm nothing."

"Liar." She hovered her mouth over mine.

"Nope," I said, my voice a low hum. "It's the truth."

"How do you figure?" Her eyes were lowered, focused completely on my mouth.

"Because I'm about to do this."

And then I kissed her.

No, more than kissed. I grabbed her by the nape and slammed my mouth to hers. Flipped her around so she was the one backed against the guardrail, then yanked one of her legs around my hip and ground myself against her so she could feel exactly how *not good* I was for her through my jeans and her paper-thin dress. I grabbed handfuls of her round, full ass, grunted into that perfect, sinful mouth, and forgot my name in the sweetness of everything that was Lea Zola.

God, I wanted to do more. All she had to do was say the word, and I would have made her outrageous, vodka-soaked goals come true. I would have yanked up her skirt and fucked her right there on the balcony, in full view of Carrera's party and half the Bronx, where any other pervert in the city with half a mind to look out their window could check out the show.

I expected her to shove me away. But she didn't. Instead, her hands were all over me too, grabbing onto my arms, flying around my neck, threading fingers into my hair so she could pull me closer, daring me to grind harder.

If she only knew, I thought again for the second time that night.

But she didn't.

And that was the crux of the matter, wasn't it?

Lea Zola was an innocent. She was a kid. Still in *high school*, as she pointed out, even if she was technically legal. She lived with her grandparents, took care of her sisters, studied for math tests, and had a whole goddamn future ahead of her that had no business being derailed by a dirty mechanic pawing her at a party in the projects.

Maybe she felt like heaven.

Maybe she tasted like home.

Maybe this was one of the greatest moments of my sad, sorry life.

None of it mattered.

Because I was still right about one thing. She was better than this place. She was better than me.

The thought rang in my head like a bell, yanking me out of the kiss. I broke away, gasping. Her own heavy breathing blew white clouds through the night air.

"Whoa," she whispered, then reached for me again.

But this time, I parried away her hands.

"No," I said. "It's time for you to go home."

Her mouth dropped open again. Her full lips were swollen from my antics. I had to force myself not to imagine what they would look like wrapped around my cock.

I failed completely.

"Are you serious?" she asked. "What do you think you're doing?"

But my mind was made up.

"I'm going back to the party," I said. "We're done here."

She opened and closed her mouth a few times before she finally spoke. "You—after that—you actually think—"

"I told you, you're better than this," I interrupted her stammering. "I lost control there for a second, but it won't happen again."

Never mind that I still had a hard-on the size of Manhattan. My mind was made up. Especially when it came to her.

"*Fine,*" she spat. "But I *will* go back in. Find someone *else* to dance with, and maybe—"

"Don't bother," I cut her off as I pulled my wallet out of my pocket.

I extracted one of my last two twenties and pressed it into her palm, ignoring the way she stared at it like I'd just passed her a packet full of magic beans or some shit. Then she looked back at me, her green eyes wet with something new.

Something like loss. Maybe a little sadness. Betrayal.

All of them painful as fuck.

But I didn't care. This was for the best.

"Take this, and get a cab home," I ordered. "And don't come to any of these parties no more. You won't be welcome. I'll make sure everyone knows that."

TEN

IN WHICH A HUNGOVER JULIET IS THE SUN

Lea

"**B**ut he can't tell you what to do!"

I stared at the notebook containing every essay I'd written since September, then finally tossed my pencil down on the thin pages. "Katie, I'm trying to work. There are two bit scholarship applications due next week. The only way we'll be able to afford for me to go to Fordham is with that money."

It was a losing battle, but I was still trying to focus on my future instead of my past. As in the night before, when Michael Scarrone had kissed my ever-loving lights out before tossing me a twenty and sending me home. Similarly, I was also trying to get rid of the worst headache I'd ever had and trying to convince Nonna I'd lost my breakfast from cramps, not the world's worst hangover.

Neither attempt was working.

Unsurprisingly, the rest of the night had been a

bust. And that was an understatement. The Tattooed Grump, as my friends had christened Michael, had hustled me out of the party and into a cab faster than Nonna shoving Joni onto the kindergarten school bus. I'd arrived home well before curfew, then slunk to my room, where Kate peppered me with questions until we both fell asleep.

At ten the next morning, she was still reeling from what had happened. I wanted to go back to sleep for at least two more days.

"I just can't believe he said that to you," Kate said as she painted her toenails purple. "He's such an arrogant jerk. Who does he think he is?"

I gagged as the scent of polish filled the room. My own nails were in desperate need of attention yet again. Linda did them for me every week, and she'd applied a fresh coat last night. But last night's tussle had chipped the bright pink paint.

"I don't know, Katie," I said. "It doesn't really matter anyway. I'm not going to let Nonno's charity project dictate my life. I was annoyed, that's all."

That was a lie. Annoyed wasn't the word for how I felt when I recalled the way Michael had grabbed my wrist. Or the way he'd kissed me. Or how he'd towed me outside, under the bridge, and over to 138th, where he forced me to wait while he hailed a cab outside Mill Brook.

He hadn't exactly liked the fact that we had to wait outside of Mill Brook until he found someone who would stop. And he really hadn't liked it when my short pink dress attracted more than a few catcalls.

"If I ever see you in a place like that again, I'll do a

fuck of a lot more than just send you home," he'd said after chasing away more of my admirers.

"Like what?" I jeered.

His gaze seared. "Like take you over my knee, contessa. Don't fuckin' test me."

I *hated* the way my skin pebbled in response, and not solely out of anger.

The cab had arrived, and Michael shoved me inside after barking my address at the driver.

"I don't make idle threats, baby girl." His glare seared across my body one last time, in a way that still wasn't totally unpleasant, much to my frustration. "Don't say I didn't warn you."

"It's fine," I told Kate, pulling myself back to reality and the Young Women's Society scholarship application that was still looking pretty damn blurry. "Nobody says we have to see each other anymore. You can bring over Nonna's charity dinners from now on."

Except I knew *that* would never happen. My sister would take one look at the "redecorating" I'd done and come right back at me with a million other questions.

Questions like "Why did you do this if you hate him?" and "Oh, you actually *care* about this one, don't you?"

And then maybe I wouldn't be able to say no without telling yet another lie.

Kate grumbled to herself. But before she could interrogate me some more, we were interrupted by a ping against our one window next to her bed.

She frowned when it happened again. "What the…?"

Keeping her toes flexed so as not to ruin her paint, she leaned over to look out the window.

I read a question about A Meaningful Experience That Informed My Character for the twentieth time that morning. Thesis One: A really stupid party. Thesis Two: Being snapped at by a hot, tattooed bad boy. Thesis Three: Being kissed by said bad boy. Thesis Four: No one cares because I'm pathetic.

"Uh…Lea? I think you should come over here."

I huffed and tossed my notebook away. "What now?"

"You have a visitor. Of sorts."

I crossed the room and got onto her bed so I could look out the window. At first, I saw nothing of note. But then I looked down into the alley between the house and the apartment building next to us. And there, waiting in his ever-present jeans, T-shirt, and a threadbare black hoodie, was Michael Scarrone.

"This guy," I muttered as I shoved up the window, letting in an icy blast of wintry air.

"Ah! Warn me first!" Kate squealed, yanking her blanket around her shoulders. She didn't move away, though, obviously eager for the show that was about to start.

I had no interest in the weather. I was too mad.

"What are you doing here?" I demanded as I leaned out the window, uncaring about the fact that I had on no makeup, my hair was a freaking mess, and I was wearing a canary-yellow bathrobe that was brighter than the sun.

Michael looked toward the street, as if he thought someone might see him standing under my window like freaking Romeo. Some Juliet I made. Hungover and pissed off instead of moon-eyed and sweet.

"We need to talk," he said.

"No, we don't. You made yourself perfectly clear last night. Now, let me make *myself* clear. Screw you."

He closed his eyes for a moment, and even from a story above him, I could see the way his lashes cast a shadow over the top of his cheekbones. I couldn't tell if he'd closed them because he was hurt or pissed off. He looked a lot like Nonno when he was trying to hold on to his temper. It almost never worked.

His eyes finally reopened. "I owe you an apology."

"Well, that's something," Kate muttered beside me.

"Yeah, something little," I said to her before calling down to him, "Too little, too late." Then I realized his right hand was covered in bandages. "What happened?"

He glanced down at his wounded paw, then shook his head. "Not now. I'm here to apologize."

"We covered that. What did you do to your hand?"

A frown emerged—one I was starting to recognize. It caused an adorable divot to appear between his dark brows and his jaw to set in a particular way that, when I was close enough to see it, made a muscle tick on the right side. It meant that he was losing patience with my attitude. It also meant I was wearing him down.

Well, good. He deserved a little humility after last night.

"Split my knuckles on some asshole's jaw after I dropped you off." He cocked his head. "Dude said the wrong thing about a pink dress. I couldn't have that."

"Oh my God, he was defending your honor!" Kate

squealed from behind me. "That's actually kind of romantic."

"More like barbaric," I informed her. "Now go away."

"Not on your life," Kate said. "This is better than Nonna's soaps."

"Lea?"

We both turned back to the window. Michael peered up at us, his expression now wide and open. I should have told him to leave. I should have told him to leave me alone.

But I couldn't look away.

"Crap," I muttered. I had a sneaking feeling I was an absolute goner. Especially when he looked at me like that.

"Kate?" Nonna called from outside the door. "I'm bringing up your laundry for you to fold, okay?"

"Noooo," Kate moaned next to me. "I don't want to miss the show."

"Take the laundry and distract her," I said. "*Please*, Katie." Then I called down to Michael. "Wait in the front, all right? I'll be down. And you can say...whatever it is you need to say."

With a quick nod, he headed back down the alley.

I closed the window and found my sister grinning at me.

"I knew you liked him," she said.

"I don't." I got off the bed and went to change out of my pajamas. "He's a Neanderthal, if you hadn't noticed."

"A hot Neanderthal, and you totally do. You just grabbed the black pants that make your ass look good."

"You're ridiculous."

I returned said pants to their drawer and went for jeans instead. That, yes, also clung to my butt like a second skin and went perfectly with the pink hoodie I traded for my bathrobe. But I wasn't going to admit that it was for him any more than were my favorite gold hoops or the way I pulled a few waves out of my top knot to frame my face. I didn't need to look homeless in front of the neighbors, after all. Or when Michael Scarrone was apparently going to grovel.

Kate laughed as I shoved my feet into my favorite purple Jordans and headed for the door. "Tell him I say hi. Right after you tell him you looooove him."

"She love who?"

Our bedroom door opened to reveal my grandmother bearing the basket of Kate's clothes, her sharp eyes darting between the two of us with the practiced eye of a seasoned parent.

"Our Father in heaven," I said grimly. "Nonna, I'm going for a walk. Gonna light a candle for Daddy."

I felt a double twinge of guilt at using the memory of my dead father and sacred prayer to distract my grandmother. Guess I was going to church for real.

It worked, though. Years of being the most well-behaved Zola kid paid off as Nonna's expression softened and her shoulders relaxed.

"My good girl," she said, balancing the basket on her hip to pat my cheek. "You want some money for the collection?"

More guilt thumped with every beat of my heart. I was definitely going to Hell.

"No, I got it," I said as I edged around her. "Do you

need anything from the market while I'm out? Or do you want me to run anything over to Nonno at the shop?"

"A butter knife," Kate called from her bed, where she was applying another coat of paint to her nails. "You know, for spreading. Since you're laying it on so thick."

I sent her my very best "you're gonna get it later" glare over my shoulder.

Kate simply cackled.

Thankfully, Nonna was too distracted by my request to process the idiom. Nothing pulled Sofia Zola's attention better than the many tasks she had to accomplish in a given day.

"I need some more pancetta for the Bolognese," she said as she set Kate's laundry on my desk chair. "Tell Ignazio, not too much fat this time, okay? And if they are still having a sale on the good tomatoes, bring more cans."

"You got it, Nonna. Love you." I pressed a kiss to her cheek.

"My good girl," she murmured again before I left.

I skipped down the stairs, ignoring my little sisters' comments as I grabbed a jacket and jetted out the front door.

Michael was waiting on the sidewalk, eyeing a neighbor down the block who was clearly eyeing him back while he took his garbage cans in from the curb.

"You gonna punch Mr. Suarez too?" I asked. "I promise he wouldn't care about my pink dress. He's mostly blind. Those glasses are for show."

Michael's nose reddened at the end when he saw

me. From embarrassment, maybe. But it was also cold, so who could tell?

"He was looking at me first," he mumbled.

I rolled my eyes, then darted down the street and away from my house before one of my nosy family members thought about peeking out the front window.

"Come on, Rocky. I just told my grandma I was going out to light a prayer candle for my dad and to pick up some groceries. I'm not about to be a liar, so you can apologize on the way."

ELEVEN

THE TIMES THEY ARE A-CHANGIN'

Lea

We made it three blocks down 187th before Michael finally got up the nerve to say something.

"Aren't—won't somebody see us over here?" he finally said. "Somebody you know?"

I glanced around the familiar shops and restaurants that made up the Little Italy of the Bronx. The sidewalks were already starting to get busy, even if it wasn't quite eleven on a Saturday. Tourists came from all over to enjoy the food and culture here. But even with the hubbub, these streets were as familiar to me as my own house, complete with countless honorary aunties and uncles haunting the storefronts and shop counters.

But what did that matter?

"Why? Are you embarrassed to be seen with me?" I asked after I waved hello to Alfredo, Nonna's third cousin, who owned a mozzarella shop.

Michael glanced at him. "No."

"Then why are you looking around like a scared rabbit?"

He turned back to me with an irritated expression. "I'm not. It's—never mind."

I shrugged, fighting the urge to push him to tell me whatever he was worried about. "Whatever. Not my problem anymore."

"Was it ever?"

I huffed. "I think you wanted to apologize. That's why you were throwing rocks at my freakin' window like a hooligan, right?"

He had the decency to look contrite. "I—yeah. I figured…"

"You figured what?" I pressed. "Spit it out."

"Then let me talk, eh?" Michael exhaled heavily.

I didn't speak, just crossed my arms and waited expectantly.

Michael chewed on his bottom lip for a moment or two, then finally continued. "Listen, last night, I didn't act right. I was an asshole, and what I did was wrong. I'm sorry. I really am."

It wasn't what I was expecting, even though he said he wanted to apologize. The truth was, I hadn't heard many of those in my life. Not good ones. My siblings only did it when forced, and my grandparents were two stubborn peas in a pod. People in my family tended to do nice things for each other when they felt bad. Fold an extra load of laundry, maybe. Take over someone's dishes for the night. If you were Nonno, bring home a bouquet of cheap roses or your wife's favorite nougat.

But somehow, this meant more.

Here was Michael, a guy who claimed to be bad all the way through, showing a rare sort of humility I couldn't help but appreciate.

"Thanks," I said, suddenly realizing I didn't actually know how to accept an apology like this one. "I… appreciate that."

One shy dimple appeared on Michael's face. "Good. I'm glad."

"But if you ever act like that again, we're done," I told him quickly before I lost my nerve. "No talking about my clothes or forbidding me from going places. No yelling at me in front of my friends. No dragging around like I'm a child. You treat me with respect, or you won't see me again. I'm serious, Michael."

His half-smile disappeared with every word out of my mouth. When I finished, he reached out to squeeze my hand.

"I know you're serious," he said solemnly. "And so am I. You're…you're kind of my only friend these days, Lea. I won't do anything else to fuck that up. I promise."

We blinked at each other for a few more minutes, like we both expected the other to say something more. Address the elephant in the room (or on the street, as it were). I wondered if he noticed that I had *not* forbidden him from kissing him again.

I certainly had. And wondered what he thought.

"Come on," I said. "I wasn't kidding about those errands."

We walked on, and when we stopped on Hoffman to wait for a break in the cars so we could cross, I caught Michael looking around and muttering under his breath.

"What's wrong now?" I asked as we started to cross. I thought we had made up.

He shook his head. "Nothing. Nothing, it's...I mean, I'm gone two years, and it feels like a different neighborhood. There's an Albanian flag over there next to Gino's. A tamale shop in front of the market. Half the neighborhood moved to Morris Park, the other half's in Westchester, Jersey, Yonkers. Wherever."

I followed his gaze to the flag hanging in the storefront next to the famous pasticceria. He wasn't wrong. "That can't be that surprising. Belmont's been changing since before we were born. It hasn't been mostly Italian for a while now."

This was another version of the same conversation I'd been hearing at the dinner table for as long as I could remember. Nonno constantly bemoaned the fact that the Belmont where he and Nonna lived for the first thirty years of their marriage was gone. The insular Italian community they remembered wasn't the one I grew up in, even if Belmont's Italian roots were still evident almost everywhere in its ten or so square blocks. I understood they missed it, but it wasn't a loss I had ever really felt.

To me, Belmont had always been a place where you were more likely to hear Spanish than Italian unless you walked into certain shops. Albanian was almost as common. And why should I have a problem with any of it? All six of the Zola kids were a product of this melting pot—thanks to our mom, we were all half-

Puerto Rican. We never thought anything of it. It simply was.

"Yeah. I know." Michael shrugged. "It's just weird thinking about how things change so quickly."

I didn't think he was talking about the neighborhood anymore.

"I'm sorry again," he said as we stopped in front of the tri-arched entry to Mary, Mother of Our Redeemer Catholic Church. "About last night, I mean."

I snorted. "Which part is still bugging you? When you went all caveman on me in the middle of a party? Or when you threatened to spank me like a little girl?"

The tips of his ears turned pink, along with his nose. This time, I knew it wasn't from the cold.

"All of it," he said. "I kind of lost it."

"Why?" I pressed. "That's what I don't understand. So I ran my mouth a little. So what?"

He kicked the toe of his boot into a bit of ice on the sidewalk. It cracked in half. "You didn't 'run your mouth.' You practically offered yourself on a platter to the entire borough."

"Yeah, but why do you even care?" I asked, even though I couldn't help but blush. "Why does it bother you so much, the idea that I would have se—"

I cut myself off as the door opened, and a squat lady who looked about a hundred years old waddled out of the church. Now, I was the one checking to make sure none of our neighbors overheard. The last thing I needed was for it to get back to Nonna that her "good girl" had been overheard talking about her sex life on Father Deflorio's steps.

"That I would *do* that," I amended after she was out

of earshot. "It's not like anyone was interested anyway. So you don't need to worry."

Michael gave me a look. One that simultaneously reminded me of how many people at that party were there for the possibility of no-strings sex...and of the fact that, at one point, the two of us had been wrapped around each other tighter than the twine around Nonna's beef roasts.

I rolled my eyes. "So you kissed me. So what? People make out at parties all the time. It doesn't mean they want to screw."

That dirty-eyed expression didn't even blink.

My cheeks grew hot.

"Stop looking at me like that," I said, as I waved across the street at Angelo del Vecchio, one of Nonno's oldest friends.

"Then stop saying dumb shit," Michael replied dryly, without a care for where we were standing. "You know exactly how you looked in that dress. And you knew exactly what most of the dudes—and probably some girls too—wanted to do to you in it. Myself included."

"Then why didn't you?"

The question leaped out of my mouth before I could stop it. Suddenly, it didn't matter that we were literally discussing my sexual valuation on the steps of my church. It had bothered me all night. If he was going to apologize, I needed to understand why he did what he did. And why he didn't do what he and I both clearly wanted.

Michael's eyes flickered with something I couldn't quite read. "You really want me to answer that?"

I crossed my arms. "I'm sick of this push and pull. You're my friend, then you're not. We fight, then we kiss, fight some more, make up. It's exhausting. You say you want me. Obviously, I was into it. So why did you stop?"

He didn't say anything for a few moments. Just looked at me like he was trying to figure out what I was thinking. His eyes darted behind me, toward the street we'd walked down, then back up to the church entrance, before returning back to me.

Finally, Michael let out a harsh sigh. "I suppose I was trying to do the right thing."

"What, protect the sad virgin? That's my call, not yours."

"No, protect *you*," he hissed. "Why do you have to make this so fucking hard? I'm trying to be a nice guy here."

"You're trying to be my daddy," I snapped. "Still. I already have a protective older brother *and* an old-school grandpa. And you're maybe three years older than me, so please cut the paternal shi—stuff. I'm not a child. I can make my own decisions about what I do with my body and who with. Including you."

"Jesus Christ, Lea."

Before I could chide him for taking the Lord's name in vain in front of an actual church, I was pulled off the steps and into an alley next to Our Redeemer. Away from anyone else who might be on their way to offer a few more prayers for sinners like him. Or me, apparently.

"I said no more dragging!" I snapped.

"I'm not. I'm helping. Now, will you please *listen*?"

He pulled me around to face him, his hand on my arm like a brand. "I know you're not a child. Believe me, I *know*."

Somehow, he'd gotten closer to me than was strictly necessary. Close enough that I could smell a faint scent of cologne or soap, stronger than the smells of pizza and tamales floating down the street, stronger than the faint whiffs of incense that always came from the church next to us.

I forced myself *not* to stare at his lips. Or to remember how soft, yet demanding, they had been last night. How his tongue had felt tangled with mine, the ache it had caused in my belly, my chest, and right between my legs.

Didn't stop him from staring at mine, though.

I swallowed. Hard. "You're looking at me like that again."

"Like what?" His gaze didn't move from my mouth.

"Like you—I don't know. Like you want to devour me or something."

He licked his lips. I only just managed not to drool.

"Maybe I do," he said, his voice so low I could hardly hear it. "I already know you taste good, contessa."

Oh, God.

My thighs squeezed together.

"So what's stopping you now?" I asked.

At that, his eyes closed, almost as if in pain. When he opened them, the obvious desire was laced with something closer to shame. He placed one palm above my shoulder, caging me against the brick wall.

"You still don't get it, do you?" His breath warmed

my cheek as he spoke. "I don't want to protect you from the world. I want to protect you from me."

I frowned, confused as much by my own reaction to him as by his words. "Oh, so we're back to that old line? What is that supposed to mean anyway?"

As if it pained him, he shoved himself away, took a step back, and ran his hand through his thick black hair. "I'm not a nice guy. I told you that. I'm not the one who'll take you out on dates, and hold your hand, and drive you around the neighborhood, and call to say good night. I live in the breakroom of your grandpa's garage. I don't have a phone or even a pager, you know that? I can't even call to ask you out properly. Not even a car to pick you up."

"What is this, nineteen fifty-five?" I demanded. "Who goes driving around the neighborhood? This is New York City. Lots of people don't have cars."

"Yeah, well, I don't even have twenty dollars to my name. I'm living on charity right now, Lea. Not even a fucking bed to call my own!"

"And how many times do I have to say it? *I don't care.*"

And I found I didn't. It was odd. How many times had I warned friends off other men because they didn't have jobs, or had petty records, or were going nowhere? Michael was waving every red flag that girls like me were trained to steer clear of. And yet, I found myself charging at each one like a bull.

"Yeah, well, I do." Michael paced back and forth around the alley, rubbing his face, his hair, and his neck as if to rid himself of something hanging over him. "You deserve better than me. You deserve the guy who'll take you to church on Sundays and act right at family dinners. You deserve all the things from whoever you give yourself to in the end, baby. But I'm not that guy, Lea. I'll *never* be that guy."

"Prove it."

It wasn't until later that I wondered why *I* cared so much. Why I was pushing him harder than I pushed anyone else. All I knew was that underneath the bickering, and the explosions, and everything else, something about this was right. Something about this was necessary.

Shrouded by a dark alley, mad as spitting cats, I still wanted him. More than anything. More than anyone.

And he wanted me too.

He just didn't believe he deserved me.

Well, I knew he was wrong about that, too. I was a Zola. Stubborn was my middle name.

"Take me on a date," I said. "A real date. It doesn't have to be fancy. It doesn't even have to cost anything. This is New York—there are plenty of things to see and do that don't cost more than a subway ride, which is on me if you don't have the cash. But all you have to do is spend some time with me. Some real time together where we aren't fighting, kissing, or doing anything else but getting to know each other. And if at the end you're miserable and convinced we're still no good together, I'll leave you alone. I'll stop bringing you food. I won't tell you what to do anymore or force you to come out. We'll just be friends whenever I do see you, but nothing too deep. The kind that never, ever kiss."

Michael stopped his pacing and looked at me. "You're serious?"

I nodded. "Dead serious."

He shook his head, then glanced back down the alley again—at what, I didn't know. "I don't know if I can do that, Lea. It's not going to work out, and I don't want to be the one to break your heart. Which I will, Lea. That's what I do. I break stuff."

"Let me be the judge of that," I said, taking a step closer to him. "I know you're not perfect. I know you have a past. But I also know that you're thoughtful, and kind, and…and sexy as hell."

He stiffened at the compliment. "I…you think that?"

I leaned in, this time enjoying the way he shuddered as my lips brushed his ear. "You weren't the only one doing the kissing last night, Michael."

Then I stepped back and traced his jaw with my finger. The coarse texture of his stubble cut into my fingertip ever so slightly. It was too easy to imagine what it might feel like…other places.

I shivered. I didn't really know what I was doing. I'd never been much of a flirt. Most guys either found me too direct or too bossy. As a result, I didn't have anywhere near the experience of most of my friends. I'd maxed out at second base, plus some heavy dry-humping in Victor's apartment when his mom was at the store. Right before he dropped me for Gina Reyes.

I shuddered and pushed the thought of my nemesis and Michael's ex-girlfriend out of my mind. If he was thinking of her at all, there was no sign of it. Not in the way he focused on me with unblinking, black-eyed intensity.

That intensity brought out a side of me I'd never known existed. One I kind of liked.

He closed his eyes and leaned into my touch, nuzzling my palm with his nose and full lips. "You're gonna be the death of me, Lea Zola. You know that?"

"I hope not," I murmured before withdrawing my hand. "I'd rather you stick with the living."

He opened his eyes, full of fear, yes, but a heavy helping of desire. "What are the chances you'll let this go?"

I shrugged. "I'd say…slim to none."

His eyes shuttered again. It seemed to be his chosen method for dealing with whatever frustration I inspired.

I kind of liked it. Especially since when they opened again, I knew I'd won.

"One date," he agreed. "*One*. And when it's over, that's it?"

"Sure, if that's what you want at the end."

"It's already what I want."

"Sure, it is," I joked.

Before I could come up with a cutting remark, I was suddenly grabbed by the waist and shoved back against the wall of the church where I'd attended Mass every Sunday of my life. One of Michael's admittedly large hands gripped my chin, forcing me to look at him and the sudden feral expression that had erased the last of his self-control.

"It's a deal," he growled. "Starting with this."

His lips were hot and rough, his tongue insistent as it practically dueled with mine. I moaned into his mouth, my hands fisting in his coat as he pressed his body into me, making his desire utterly clear against my hip.

On holy ground.

But this couldn't be wrong. It felt too good to be a sin.

As suddenly as he had begun, the kiss was over.

"I—who—what?" I gasped, my breath spilling into the air in wintry plumes. What had just happened?

"Told you I don't do anything the right way," he said with a smirk, as he pushed off the wall and started back toward the street. "That's your goodbye kiss, Tess. Now go say your prayers and get your nonna's groceries. I'll be waiting for you at seven, right outside your house."

Breathlessly, I nodded. I'd need a few moments before I headed into the church, though. Damn, but the boy could kiss.

"And, Lea?"

I turned toward Michael, who was about to step back out onto the sidewalk. "Yeah?"

"Maybe don't tell your family who's taking you out tonight," he said. "The fewer people who know about the mistake you're making, the better."

I frowned. I wanted to ask again why he cared but decided I didn't want to fight again. Not with his kiss still tingling on my lips.

Not when we would be able to "fight" properly later.

Yes, I decided as he disappeared around the corner that a good fight for our first date sounded perfect. I already knew he couldn't walk away from one. Especially when it was with me.

TWELVE

HOW IS THIS PICKING ME UP?

Lea

Tap. Tap. Tap.

I sat at my desk-turned-vanity, putting the final touches on my hair with a flatiron when the familiar sound of rocks hitting my window came for the second time that day.

I glanced at the clock on my bedside table. It was six fifty, and I had ten minutes before Michael was supposed to be picking me up.

Tap. Tap. Tap.

I huffed and got up to go to the window and was immediately struck by déjà vu.

It was him, of course. He'd swapped out the hoodie for the white button-up and wool coat he'd worn to my grandparents' the other night. It was quickly becoming evident that Michael had two, maybe three sets of clothes besides the coveralls he wore at the garage. I liked this one the best.

"You ready?" he called once I'd lifted the window and popped my head out.

"Are you serious?" I called back. "How is this 'picking me up'? This is supposed to be a real date, Michael. Otherwise, it doesn't count."

"Oh, it's gonna count," he said with a delicious smirk. "Come down when you're ready, contessa. I'll be waiting out front."

He didn't wait for me to answer; he just took off down the alley back toward the main street. With a huff, I closed the window.

"'Come down when you're ready,'" I muttered. "How about *you* come in like a gentleman?"

I put in my earrings and took one last look at myself in the mirror Kate and I kept over our bedroom door. I looked good. Nothing fancy—the black pants Kate had teased me about this morning, the Timberlands I'd gotten for Christmas, and my pink puffer jacket that made my waist look tiny. But I'd done my eyeliner like the night before and had taken some extra time to iron my hair perfectly straight. Michael said this was our only date, but I wasn't going to make it easy for him to walk away.

Nonna and Nonno were enjoying *aperitivi* in the kitchen, overseeing Joni and Marie as the girls drew and bickered at the dining table. Kate had gone to a friend's house for the night, and I was guessing that Frankie was lost in a book, taking advantage of having the room she shared with the two littles to herself for once.

It was the perfect moment to pop out of the house without causing a ruckus.

Michael was pacing on the sidewalk and practically jumped when I opened the door.

"What are you doing?" I asked. "This is not how you start a proper date."

"Lea?" Nonna's voice sounded from within. "Did you open the door?"

Michael looked absolutely terrified. "Tell them you're going to a friend's. I'll wait."

I frowned. "Why? My grandparents already know you. You should come in to say hello."

He shook his head several times. "Nah, better not to give them the wrong idea. We're only doing this once, remember?"

I huffed. This was more than annoying. Eventually, I'd have to teach the boy some manners, but we'd get there. I was already sure of it. "Whatever you say. Wait here."

I ducked back inside and walked into the kitchen.

Joni's eyes grew as big as the moon. "Woah, your *hair*. Where are *you* going?"

I ignored her and called to Nonna, who was blushing while her husband murmured sweet nothings into her ear. Or, knowing my rascally grandfather, not so sweet.

Good, they were a little sauced. That would work in my favor.

"Nonno, I'm going out with a friend. I won't be out late."

Nonna opened her mouth as if to argue but was stopped when Nonno cut her off with a quick Italian phrase. I wasn't even close to fluent, but I knew enough to decipher that his meaning was something like, "With fewer mice in the house, the cats can play."

I was pretty sure he meant the two of them. Cute but gross.

Nonna took another sip of her cocktail. "*Sì, sì,* my love. Back by curfew, okay?"

"No problem, Nonna. Love you."

I didn't even get a response—the two of them were too busy canoodling in the kitchen corner while Joni and Marie made gagging noises at the table.

Outside, Michael was pacing the sidewalk like a cat, but he stopped when he heard the door open again.

"All right, James Bond," I said as I skipped down the steps, hopping over the third one that squeaked. "Your dirty little secret is safe. They were too into flirting with each other to wonder where I was going."

His face twisted like he'd eaten something bad. "Doesn't that make you want to go back in? You should be out with someone who wants to show you off, not hide from your family, don't you think?"

My stomach flipped at his words, but I ignored the fact that he was actually right. That couldn't be how he *actually* felt. Not if he was saying it out loud.

"So, what are we doing?" I asked, as I took his hand without waiting for him to offer.

He looked down at our joined palms, then back at me. Then he seemed to give up the idea of fighting, instead opting to tuck my hand into his jacket pocket along with his. His thumb brushed the inside of my palm. I shivered despite the warmth of my jacket.

"I had some ideas," he said. "Nothin' fancy, but more than walk. And before you offer again, it's on me." His mouth curved into a shy smile. "I got paid today." He held up a plastic bag that was obviously full of something for the two of us.

I perked. "You should be saving that money."

"Nah, I got it."

I followed him to the corner of 187th, where a yellow taxi sat, engine purring. I didn't realize it was for us until Michael strode forward to open the door.

"A cab?" I asked. "Michael, no. Come on, let me help. I have a little money from babysitting and helping Nonno at the shop."

"Jesus, Lea, fuckin' *stop*."

To my surprise, I found myself obeying the curt order. I swallowed but made no move. I wasn't sure what he wanted me to do right now.

Michael shook his head as he opened the back door of the car. "Get in. Let me do this my way, all right?"

I recognized a man's pride. I'd seen it in my nonno's face too often not to. It was a quality he often said too many men lacked. Something he respected in others.

For the first time, I considered the possibility that Nonno had hired Michael as more than a favor to our priest.

I got in. He slid in beside me and called out directions to the driver, who stepped on it so abruptly that I was jerked back in my seat. Quickly, Michael reached around me, nearly caging my body against the frayed leather seats.

He was so...close. His body suddenly seemed *much* bigger than it had before. I felt the heat pouring off his skin, registered the slight scratch of his chin against my cheek, and caught the scent of men's body wash, a little bit of motor oil, and something that was indescribably and deliciously *him*.

"I—what are you doing?" I asked, though I could barely get the words out.

"Your seat belt," he murmured, breath warm against my ear while the familiar click barely registered in the back of my mind.

Then, just as quickly, he sat back in his seat and offered a sly grin as he fastened his own belt.

I almost melted right there.

"Th—thanks," I stuttered before turning to the window.

I felt like I was losing the upper hand.

And I wasn't sure I liked it.

We sat in silence as the car drove through the Bronx Park, most of which was completely black in the dark of the night. Michael seemed content to stare out his window, unwilling to make conversation or even look at me. Every time I peeked at him, he didn't look back at me, much to my frustration. But it gave me some time to observe him. How he'd taken a minute to comb his hair as he had for dinner with my grandparents. And how he'd spot-cleaned his black boots, which looked shinier than they ever had. His white shirt collar was open a bit more, revealing bits of the tattoo I was sort of dying to see in full, but also a silver box chain I hadn't noticed before. It shone whenever a streetlight caught it, but it wasn't anything close to some of the chains even kids at my high school liked to wear. Unostentatious and quietly beautiful. Exactly like him.

"Are you going to say *anything* to me tonight?" I finally demanded after about ten minutes of silence.

"Or are you planning to sit there like a mute the entire time?"

The car had been winding its way west, away from Belmont. I realized I'd been too lost in studying him to notice where we were going. He could be taking me anywhere.

Michael turned to me, black brows raised in mild surprise, like he'd only just realized I was there.

"Would that put you off, Tess?" he asked quietly. "Make you do the right thing and leave me alone?"

I examined him for a long moment. I knew a dare when I heard one.

"I've got four sisters, Scarrone," I informed him. "If you think a pathetic little silent treatment is going to make me tap out, you have severely underestimated this woman. I win that contest every. Single. Time."

A full-throated laugh burst out of him, like confetti on New Year's or balloons falling at a graduation. It was so joyful. A momentary but complete celebration that made my skin prickle and dance, and every cell in my body wake up in response.

My God, he was *beautiful* when he smiled.

"Christ, Lea," he said, wiping away the tears of mirth. "You are too damn much, you know that?"

I smirked. I didn't particularly like being the butt of an unspoken joke, but I did like breaking down that wall. Because Michael Scarrone had definitely erected walls around himself. More than walls, really. He lived all alone in a fortress of his own making. But now, I'd found a crack in the mortar.

As quickly as it came, the light in his eyes was gone. I wanted it back. It made me want to do more than fight with Michael Scarrone. For the first time, I found myself wanting to make him happy, just to see that joy again on his otherwise too-somber face.

Before I could say anything more, the taxi came to a stop. We were no longer in the Bronx but had crossed the Harlem River into Manhattan. The car was right outside the subway station on 207th, outside the 1 train, the number blazing in a red ball on the sign.

Michael paid the cabbie, slid out of his side of the car, and then quickly jogged around to open my door for me. There I found him standing, hand extended.

"Come on, contessa," he said, his voice a deep growl in the night. "We've got a train to catch. And don't worry, I promise I'll talk on the way."

THIRTEEN

IT'S JUST WATER UNDER THE FERRY

Michael

The second we got onto the train, I knew that this night was a mistake. Actually, I knew it the second Lea popped her head out of her bedroom window after I'd tossed pebbles at it. A girl like her—smart, beautiful, loyal to her family, obviously going places—and all I've got to offer are rocks. I should have obeyed her nonno's orders and walked away right then. Or better yet, never come in the first place.

But I told myself this way was easier. I already knew Lea. Tell her she can't have something, and she'll work that much harder to get it. That saying about how behind every great man is a strong woman? She was the type they were talking about.

Or she would be. If I could only get out of her way.

When she came out to the street, though, I couldn't take one step away from the girl. That's when I knew I was fucked.

She looked beautiful, dressed in tight pants, a winter coat, and dark hair that fell down her back like satin. Her full mouth smirked when she caught me glancing at her ass, and the twinkle in those emerald greens made me feel like I couldn't walk straight.

Like I said. Fucked.

We sat on the train, wedged together on those tiny seats, while the train car grew increasingly full with every stop toward the city. I could feel the heat of her leg pressed against mine, but I still kept my hands white-knuckle gripping my own knees. And it felt wrong, all wrong. Not to touch her. Not to kiss her. Not to let every dude in this place know she was mine.

Wrong, just fuckin' *wrong*.

"You're still quiet," she told me, direct as ever, while I wondered how I'd gotten myself into this mess.

But this couldn't happen. I was literally forbidden by my boss—in a job I was damn lucky to have—to have anything to do with this very person. But instead of following Zola's rule number four, I'd been badgered into a date with the apple of his eye. And I couldn't bring myself to sabotage this date the way I needed to.

I swallowed, looking up to find, of course, a subway crime PSA advertising Rikers fucking Island.

Of course.

I'd never be able to escape the last two years. Never see beyond it. Never be anything more.

I supposed it was a good reminder. A clear sign of what I had to do. The truth was about to set me free from this stubborn woman. Problem was, with her, I actually wanted to be a captive.

"I'm thinking," I said with a sigh, then nodded at the ad.

Darkness curtained her face when she followed my glance. "Oh."

Her voice was softer than I'd expected, sadness clouding her features. Her eyes traced the outline of the imposing structure behind a picture of a kid in hand-cuffs. It was a somber reminder of the world we lived in, a world that pulled people apart rather than bringing them together.

God, I hoped she never had to know more about that world than she had to.

Lea's hand reached out and brushed over mine, her touch sending an electric jolt through my body. She was looking for an invite. I pulled my palm into my lap and looked away.

"I asked around about you, you know."

My head jerked back toward her. "You did what?"

That was the last thing I expected to hear.

She shrugged. "It was already big news around the neighborhood. School, etcetera. Your ex-girlfriend was in one of my classes last year, you know."

"I—you know Gina?" I definitely wasn't expecting that.

She gave me another look that said I was right to feel like an idiot. "Belmont's not that big. Of course, I know Gina Reyes. We, um…we go back."

Something in her voice told me it wasn't in a good way. Which shouldn't have surprised me. Gina was hot —all that nineteen-year-old me really cared about when we were hooking up—but she had claws. Sharp ones.

"Well, whatever they're saying, it isn't true," I said.

"Especially her. We don't talk ever. We barely even did when we were hanging out."

Lea's face flushed the color of a pink rose as she obviously imagined what exactly Gina and I were doing if not talking.

Shit. Maybe I'd fuck this up without even trying. Maybe all I had to do was say more insensitive shit like that.

The problem was, I couldn't bring myself to hurt Lea on purpose.

"So you're not planning to get back together with her?" Her voice was small. Tentative. And the look on her face made me want to get on my knees right then and beg her forgiveness.

"Fuck. No," I said definitively. "Not in a million fuckin' years."

"Why?"

She didn't sound jealous. Just curious. Like she knew very well how hot Gina was—she and the rest of Belmont. And sure, I knew it too. Gina Reyes was the girl every kid on the block wanted to get with, so why wouldn't I go back to hitting that on the regular if she was practically begging for it?

Those green eyes, though. No sign of envy, but they speared just the same.

"Why would I go back for that mess when I got perfection right here?" I blurted out.

I had no business talking to her like that. But I couldn't help the utter fucking bliss I felt when she glowed at my kind words. Things I shouldn't have said but somehow meant completely.

It occurred to me then that nothing felt better than

this moment. Maybe nothing in my life would ever feel better than making Lea Zola, a girl I barely knew, shine with happiness.

"They say you stole that car to pay your best friend's debts," she said after a moment or two. "Were they lying about that?"

I stared at my hands, no longer able to bear looking at that goddamn ad or feeling like she could see right through me. I wrapped the plastic handle around my fingers until the tips turned white. "I already told you that story."

"Answer the question, Michael."

I looked up at the cracked plastic ceiling of the train car. Jesus, couldn't anything in this fucking city be perfect?

Well, one thing was. And she was sitting right next to me.

"Paul Reyes was never my best friend," I mumbled. "So I guess they are lying."

Lea's eyes flew open. "You stole the car for Paul Reyes?"

I sighed. "Gina's brother, yeah. But it was really for her. She said he needed help. Begged me to do something. So I did the only thing I could think of."

It was the easiest way to describe the situation without saying things I shouldn't. And Civics were easy cars to lift. Everyone knew that. It was why they ended up in chop shops more than any others.

"He was in with some heavies around the neighborhood. They agreed to a trade—three cars in exchange. Got the one before I got caught."

I shook my head. I didn't mention that Paul had

come sniffing around on behalf of the Mancusos again, trying to make good on the rest of that bargain. Me, I considered the matter closed. I hadn't ratted on anyone. I'd served my time. They got two years of my life and my silence instead of two more shitty Hondas.

Finally, I turned, expecting to see disappointment. But her face was utterly unreadable.

"I knew you were a liar," she said at last. Then crooked a smile that brightened my cold, black heart.

I raised one brow. "You think so, Tess?"

She smirked. "'Because I wanted to.' Liar." Her finger pushed into my chest. "I knew you were a good guy at heart, Michael Scarrone. You can't fool me."

I couldn't help but feel a mix of relief and confusion. Lea saw through my tough exterior and recognized the flickering ember of goodness within me. And with every smile, every mild push to be something better, it was like she was blowing on that ember, coaxing it back into a flame.

Lea's touch lingered on my chest, her finger pressing against my heart. It was as if she was trying to assure herself that the spark she saw was real, that I wasn't just another disappointment waiting to happen.

And in that moment, I made a silent promise—I wouldn't let her down.

"You're something else, Lea Zola," I told her, my voice barely above a whisper. "No one's ever said things like that to me."

Her eyes locked on to mine, her gaze unwavering and strong. She took my hand in hers, and this time I let her.

"Maybe it's about time someone did."

I couldn't find it in myself to argue.

The subway came to its final stop, jolting us back to reality.

Lea glanced around as the doors opened. "Battery Park?"

"Nah," I said, keeping her hand in mine as I guided her off the train. "We have one more ride to take."

She quieted as I guided her through the station. God, that I could take her someplace better. That I could afford more than a two-dollar subway fare for the one date we had. That I could show her something nicer than a rat-infested subway platform and a free boat ride.

But this was my life. And I was trying to make the best of it.

"We're going to Staten Island?" she asked as we came to the edge of the ferry dock right as the next boat was coming in.

I squeezed her hand and looked down at her. "We won't be getting off. But I thought...maybe you might like...well, I brought us dinner. For a cruise. So to speak."

She looked at me for a long moment, then down at the plastic bag, then back up at me.

What the hell was she thinking? That I was stupid for thinking this would work? That a ride on a subway and then the Staten Island Ferry wasn't an actual date, just an exercise in public transit? That I'd broken my promise and fucked up yet again?

The ferry came to a stop. The attendants removed the chains, and we waited while the riders exited before we could get on.

When I got up the courage to look at her again, I found her grinning up at me. That smile. My God. It was going to be the fucking end of me.

"It's perfect, Michael," she said as she squeezed my arm. "I can't think of anything better."

Relief washed over me in waves that matched those on the river.

As we stepped onto the ferry, the cool breeze coming off the water kissed our cheeks. It was cold enough to snow, but the night was clear. Almost clear enough that you could spot stars beyond the halo of light that enclosed the city. It was as if the universe was conspiring to create a moment only for us.

I guided Lea inside the sheltered portion of the ferry, and we took a seat on a cold metal bench. Paint was chipping off the edges from so many years of use, but Lea treated it like a throne. She watched as I spread a dish cloth between us—one of the ones she had gotten me, covered with cartoon watermelons—then pulled out two sandwiches wrapped in red checkered paper and a few bottles of Coke.

"Hope you like turkey," I said. "They gave me two for one at the market."

"Enzo's?" she asked as she took a sandwich and unwrapped it, revealing layers of freshly sliced turkey, salami, provolone, and all the other makings of a good Italian sandwich on fresh bread.

I nodded. "It's the best."

"It certainly is." Her eyes closed in bliss as she took a bite. "Mmm," she hummed appreciatively. "Enzo's sandwiches are amazing."

"Christ," I muttered, transfixed by the sight of

complete and total ecstasy on her face. And by the very dirty thoughts it was sending through my mind. Just like that, I was hard as a fucking rock.

"Aren't you going to eat?" She gestured at the food between us.

I smiled. "I am." I unwrapped my own sandwich and took a bite. "Shit, that is good."

I meant it too. I loved Lea's cooking and her grandma's too. But there were certain tastes that haunted me when I was in the joint. Enzo's sandwiches were one of them.

"Did you know Enzo is my nonna's second cousin?"

"Get out of the city," I teased her. Was there anyone in Belmont her grandmother wasn't related to? Then again, in Belmont, any Italians still left were second or third cousins to everyone else.

Lea gaped, sandwich held in mid-air. "Oh my God, did you actually quote *Perfect Strangers*?"

I grinned. "You remember that show?"

"It was my dad's favorite." A shadow crossed her face. "Funny, I haven't thought of that in years. But he used to tune in every Friday at eight, right after we were supposed to be in bed. When my mom was gone— which was most of the time—Matthew and I would watch with him and put ourselves to bed, though. Kate was maybe three or four, I think? Marie and Joni wouldn't have even been born yet, probably."

"So you didn't always live with your grandparents?" I wondered before I could stop.

Her face darkened a bit more, and immediately, I regretted asking. I actually knew a bit of this story now that I thought about it. I was only a little bit older than

Lea's brother, and even though I was too involved in my own shit to really care at the time, I still recalled the rumors about the Zola kids' parents. Someone died. Someone went to jail. But I didn't remember who was who or what exactly happened.

But instead of changing the subject, I found myself waiting for the answer. Lea Zola had a way of getting secrets out of me I'd never had any interest in sharing. I wanted a few of hers, too.

"My parents met in high school," she said after she took a sip of her Coke. "Young, you know. Like us. My mom…well, I don't really know. Nonna says she was no good. A bad influence on Daddy. He used to work at the shop with Nonno, I guess, and he was supposed to take over so Nonno could retire one day. But then he met Mami, and…I like to think they fell in love, you know?"

I offered a smile. Of course she'd want to think that. And maybe it was true, too. Her parents had six kids together, after all. That didn't come from nothing.

It was funny, though. The way she said it didn't sound like she thought love was a good thing.

She took another bite of her sandwich, chewed thoughtfully, and swallowed again before she continued. "Anyway, they had the first three of us quick. Matthew, me, then Kate. Mattie and I are only a year and a half apart. Kate's not quite two years younger than me. We share a room."

"I figured when she was at the window with you. You look alike, you know."

Lea offered a funny little smile. "We all got Daddy's hair and our mom's eyes. Black and green."

"Plus, you got something special just yours," I put in.

That earned me a fucking adorable half-smile while her eyelashes swept across her cheek. But she was still in storytelling mode.

"Mami…had a problem—has a problem," she corrected herself. "She drinks too much. Once she passed out while my dad was at work, and when he came home, he found us trying to cook rice on the stove. Mattie was only six. We almost burned the place down, and she was still asleep. At least, that's what Mattie says. I don't really remember. But after that, Daddy took us with him to Nonno and Nonna's so Mami could straighten herself out. It took a while. A few years, actually." She shook her head wistfully. "I think about those years with my dad, and I miss it. And then I feel bad for missing it, you know? Because she wasn't there. And she's my mother. I'm supposed to love her no matter what."

"Well, she was supposed to take care of you, no matter what. So honestly, I don't think you owe her anything."

I couldn't help the bitterness that touched the statement. Sure, this story wasn't particularly unique. Shit, it wasn't even that unique between the two people on this bench. But for some reason, the idea of anyone abandoning Lea Zola in any way got to me good. I ignored the possibility that it came from the overwhelming urge I felt to take care of her myself.

Lea didn't answer, just looked out one of the open windows on the other side of the ferry, where the Statue of Liberty stood bright and tall across the water.

"But there's three more of you," I prompted. "So, they must have gotten back together."

She offered a sad smile. "They did. Mami actually got sober for a while. I remember when we moved back in with her. She was so happy to have us, and it felt so good to be with her again." She blinked wistfully. "Daddy was happy too. I remember he was kissing her all the time back then."

"How old were you?"

"Oh…maybe seven or eight? My sister Frankie was born pretty soon after. And then a few years after that, they had Marie and Joni."

Another shadow crossed her face.

"Most kids would be happy with their parents back together," I said, even though it was a lie. There were plenty of families that shouldn't be together.

"They weren't…great years," she admitted. "We lived in an apartment maybe ten blocks from my grand-parents. All us kids in one bedroom, the babies in the other with my parents. It was…chaotic."

"Chaotic, how?" I asked, even though the famil-iarity was starting to prickle my skin. I knew exactly what it was like to spend a childhood on floors, couches, or shared beds. The idea of Lea having to go through that made me sick.

But somehow, I needed to know the rest. I needed to know all of any story she wanted to tell.

"They fought a lot," she said, as she held her Coke between both of her hands, like the cold bottle would somehow warm them. "Mami started drinking again. Mattie says she had other addictions too, but I don't know. I never saw any of that. But my dad started drinking again, too, maybe to be with her. So Matthew and I were in charge most of the time. Doing our best to keep things together."

It was another puzzle piece that clicked in to place. I could imagine it all perfectly—a two-bedroom apartment crammed with kids, like too many others in the Bronx. Parents who had no business having them in the first place overwhelmed with responsibility that they passed off to their young children. I had never known Matt Zola that well—only that he was a smart kid, the girls liked him, and he got into fights a lot.

Now that I thought about it, he always seemed to carry the damn world on his shoulders. It made sense, knowing this story. Just like Lea's pushy personality and opinionated sass made sense too. She'd been in charge her whole damn life, whether she wanted to be or not. In a fucked-up way, I realized she wouldn't push so much if she didn't care.

Which meant Lea Zola cared about me.

"Anyway, after Joni came, things got really bad," she continued after another bite of her sandwich. "Mami couldn't handle her and Marie at all. I think maybe they were accidents. Or maybe we all were."

"I don't think so."

One black brow arched in that sly way I was starting to love. "Oh? And how would you know, Michael?"

I tipped my head. "Because you could never be an accident, Tess. Not when you're so damn…"

She leaned closer with a dare in her eyes. "I'm what?"

I couldn't help but stare at her lips. She sucked on

them when she was thinking, making them even more swollen. Even more kissable.

"Perfect," I murmured before I could help myself.

She flushed. And the fuck if I didn't want to rip open her coat to see how far down that gorgeous pink went.

Fuck.

She was staring at my lips, and for a second, I thought she might kiss me again. Instead, she tore her gaze away and took the biggest bite of her sandwich she could manage.

"And now?" I finally asked. I wanted the story to be over so I could do…something. Kiss her. Hold her. Do something else that would take her mind out of this dark place and put a smile on her face like she deserved.

"Now my dad is dead," she said bluntly. "And my mom is in jail for it."

That made me do a double take. I didn't realize the two things were connected. "She…"

"She didn't murder him if that's what you're about to suggest." Her voice was suddenly choked and defensive. Obviously, she'd heard that rumor a time or two.

I held up my hands. "Whoa, hey. I didn't think she did."

That was a lie, yeah, but I wasn't going to tell her that.

Lea relaxed a bit, though her shoulders were still tense. "I—it was a really bad time. I wasn't even thirteen when the police and a social worker came to our door. We were watching reruns of *Who's the Boss?* I can still remember Tony Micelli saying, 'Ay-oh! Oh-ay!' like you just did, while the cop told us about how my parents had too much to drink, but my mom took the wheel anyway and killed my dad and the other driver and passenger in the accident. Orphaned her six kids for a joyride to Atlantic City."

"And they sent you to your grandparents?"

I hoped to God they did. I knew exactly how fucked up—and slow—the New York child welfare system could be. It was too easy to imagine their case worker passing them off to a temporary foster home when they had a perfectly good place to stay, with loving grandparents ten blocks away. And the idea of Lea living in some of the places I had as a kid? That made me feel fucking lethal.

Thankfully, she shook her head. "We'd already been there for a few weeks, actually. But yeah. Since they already had a record of us in their care, they released us back to Nonno within an hour or so. It was still scary, though. And sad. Mami was convicted of three counts of manslaughter since she killed the other car's passengers too. The judge gave her twenty years."

We didn't say anything for a long time, just munched on the rest of our sandwiches. The ferry docked at Staten Island, and for a moment, I considered leading her off the boat. That wasn't the original plan. The ferry ride itself was the date; dinner on the water was the best I could afford. Lea seemed to know it too, since she made no move to get off with the rest of the passengers.

But for a moment, I wanted to take her away. We seemed so far from the city that had taken so much from both of us, where responsibility and harsh pasts awaited us, that I wanted to continue on. Run as far as we could possibly go.

But when she looked at me, her eyes sparkling brighter than any star hidden over the city ever could, there was something else there I'd never known.

Hope, shining bright and true.

Misguided, maybe. Especially if she had hope for me. But totally addictive.

So I did the only thing I could do in a moment like that. I slipped a hand around her neck, buried my fingers in the warm thicket of hair, and pulled her close.

"I'm sorry," I mumbled against her lips.

And then I kissed her like I'd been meant to my entire fucking life.

FOURTEEN

THAT CERTAINLY CHANGES EVERYTHING

Michael

We didn't really talk much on the ferry ride back to Manhattan. Or on the 1 train that chugged up the length of the island. Or at Columbus Circle while we waited for the B-D line transfer. Or in the seat we found in the last train car all the way back to Fordham Heights, a subway stop much closer than the line we'd taken downtown.

She didn't seem to notice. We were too busy communicating in…other ways.

Seriously, though. I hadn't made out that intensely with a girl since Juliana de Soto's birthday party in the eighth grade. There was something so pure about kissing and nothing more.

Not that I didn't want to do a hell of a lot more. The problem with kissing Lea Zola was that once I started, I really couldn't stop. The conversation, the sandwiches, hell, the damn ferry—it all had broken a dam deep inside me, and now something was flowing right into her, hot and fast.

She felt so damn good in my arms, warm and soft and welcoming to my touch. Her lips were more suckable than candy, and the slick of her tongue slipping around mine was a version of heaven I'd never even considered.

The girl was voracious. And, apparently, shameless, which suited me just fine. She didn't care that we were in public places—she seemed to need me as much as I craved her.

Underneath the tough, prim face she showed the rest of the world was a vixen, a passionate creature I got the feeling was rarely let out. After our conversation tonight, I understood why. Suddenly, kissing her, holding her, giving in to the burning desire I felt for Lea Zola didn't make me feel like a sinner but more like a savior.

Lea carried the damn world for nearly everyone in her family. She needed to let loose. Have a space to be free. Be a little bad, like most eighteen-year-olds should have a chance to be.

If I could keep her safe at the same time, maybe I was actually doing her a favor.

Or maybe that's what I was telling myself so I could keep devouring that luscious mouth like it was the dessert I'd forgotten to bring.

"Approaching Fordham Road."

The blare of the conductor's voice through the blown-out speakers only partially registered in between kisses.

"Michael."

She was lucky, really, that at that moment, I'd taken the opportunity to taste the delicate skin under her jaw. It allowed her to look up at the light board at the top of the train that informed us of the next stop.

"Michael." Her fingers grabbed my hair at the base of my neck and tugged.

"Mmmph."

She tasted like honey. Like a flower, with some mild perfume in her hair and on her skin. Something that reminded me of honeysuckles and lilies and some other flower I'd only ever seen at the New York Botanical Garden on a field trip when I was seven.

"Michael, this is our stop."

With a harsh, tight breath, I managed to drag my lips from her skin. When our eyes met, it was all I could do not to kiss her again. She was fucking glowing, her long hair pleasantly mussed, lips swollen, cheeks reddened. Smiling, flushed, and so damn beautiful, it made my chest hurt.

The doors opened with the familiar chime.

I stood up and pulled her with me. "Come on, Tess."

We stumbled onto the platform and then up to the surface. But the spell of the underground was broken as we walked back to Belmont. Lea remained quiet, her small hand gripping mine while she looked around the neighborhood like she hadn't made this walk almost every day of her life.

I didn't make much of an effort to talk either. Dread lodged further in my belly with every step. Toward her house. Toward the garage. Toward all the reasons why this wasn't going to work.

I'd allowed myself one night with Lea Zola. Given her a simple date of takeout sandwiches on the Staten Island Ferry, a few hours of subway rides, and a whole lot of making out. It wasn't much, but it was probably one of the best nights of my life.

And now it was almost over.

I hated that it was almost over.

The scent of pizza and the sounds of wine-soaked laughter told me we had reached Belmont before I noticed any of the Italian signs or flags still hanging in a few of the shopfronts. With a lead-filled heart, I stopped on the corner of 187th and Hughes, then pulled her to face me. I didn't dare walk her all the way home. Not with the chance of my boss spotting us from the window or anyone else in her family. From here, I could see when she got to her doorstep down the street.

"I had a good time, Lea," I said quietly. Because I couldn't help it, I pushed a bit of her hair behind her ear and ran my finger over the downy skin below it before pulling back.

Lea frowned. "What is it? Is something wrong?"

I shrugged. "We're back."

Realization spread over that gorgeous face, and Christ, it made my chest hurt. I don't want the night to end either, baby.

Especially when I knew it was for good.

"So I'll see you…"

Four simple words shouldn't have sounded so final. But they really did.

"Are you kidding?" Her bright green gaze boomeranged between me and her house. "That's it?"

I swallowed hard. "I—yeah. It's the end of the night. I'm supposed to drop you at home, aren't I?"

She looked at her watch, then back at me. "It's barely ten o'clock, Michael."

"Don't you...don't you have a...?"

"Curfew?" she finished like it was a dirty word. Her hand found her hip, and once again, I was on the receiving end of her glare.

"Well, you are in high school," I said lamely, though I was unable to meet her eyes when I said it. Just acknowledging the fact made me feel like a dirty old man.

"I do, but it's more like a guideline than a rule," she returned. "Because I'm also an adult, in case you forgot. My grandparents certainly haven't."

I wasn't so sure about that, given her nonno's warning to me when I met him, but I didn't say so. I'd already crossed too many lines tonight.

"If this were a date with someone else, would you end it now?" Lea demanded.

I should have said yes. But I couldn't lie. "No."

"Well, then. I want some dessert," she said.

I sighed. "I'm out of cash, Lea. And before you say it, no, I don't want you to pay."

She huffed. "Fine. No dessert. But I would like to... talk...some more."

The new flush of pink on her cheeks told me she definitely wasn't thinking of conversation when she said that.

And now my jeans were tight all over again.

"Lea," I started, though she was already pulling me close.

"You said you'd take me on a real date." Her hands slipped into my jacket and around my waist. "If you were with someone else, someone older, someone who was obviously interested in continuing somewhere private, what would you do?"

Her hips pressed into mine. There was no way she couldn't feel the effect she had on me right there, against her leg.

Fuck, I was trying to be a gentleman here, but she wasn't making it easy.

"I'd ask her upstairs," I admitted, as her hands played idly with my shirt. I couldn't stop myself from wrapping my arms around her shoulders. Our lips were almost touching. Almost. Not quite. "For a drink, maybe. Or coffee."

Vaguely, I wondered if I could get the shitty coffee machine in her grandpa's office working. Or if Lea even drank shitty coffee at all.

"And then what?" Her lips brushed mine.

Someone on the street laughed. It was a man's laugh. Someone older.

I started at the sound and tried to pull away. I shouldn't be out here like this with her. Where anyone could see, let it get back to—

"Adult, Michael," Lea interrupted my thoughts as she took my chin and pulled my face back to hers. "And then what would you do?"

When she popped up onto her tiptoes and caught my ear between her teeth, every reservation I had flew out of my mind as quickly as the taxi that passed us. I shuddered as the wet heat of her tongue slipped along the lobe.

"And then I'd... fuck, Lea... I'd worship this ass with my palm before...I... Fedthislusciousmouthmydick and paintedyourprettytitswithmycome—*fuck*!"

As her teeth bit lightly into my ear, the words spilled out all at once, like I'd been holding them in for weeks, not hours.

Her breath caught. For a second, I wondered if I'd ruined it for real this time. Lea said she wanted reality, wanted a real man, but she was still legitimately an innocent, no matter what her tongue could do. She had no idea what kind of filth she was releasing in my mind. What kind of dirty things I wanted to do to her perfect body.

Her mouth trailed over my jaw, then landed on mine. And it was like we were right back on that train, drinking up every drop of heat we could, acting like we were each other's Last damn Suppers.

Well, maybe we were. At least, she was for me.

It was only a kiss, but I already knew that no one else would ever compare to the angel in my arms.

"I said I wanted a real date," she whispered. "So I guess you'd better take me back to the breakroom and follow through with your plans."

"Jesus." I grunted before I took her mouth again. "Fuck it. Let's go."

Her hand clasped in mine, we raced up the familiar blocks back to the garage, where I prayed none of the mechanics would be working late. Everything was dark when I unlocked the door, guided her around the unfinished cars, and escorted her up the stairs to the room above the garage.

Every alarm bell in my head was going off as I

opened the door to the space I couldn't even call my own. But I ignored them all the second Lea jumped into my arms.

As our lips met in a fiery collision, her fingers tangled in my hair and clutched me even closer. A low growl from deep in my chest echoed in the darkness. Christ, she made me feral. She herself was a damn wildcat. From angel to animal in less than a second.

"Take me," she whispered against my lips as she took my hands and moved them to her very perfect ass. "Do what you said, right here above the garage. Do it all and m-more."

I groaned. It was taking everything I had not to devour her whole. Especially when she was turning us both around, letting me subconsciously stumble us both over to the futon, which thankfully I'd made before leaving. Her legs buckled, and we fell onto the makeshift bed. I pushed her jacket off her shoulders, pulled at the hem of her shirt, then lost my breath completely as she lifted it over her head and lay back on my pillows in nothing but her simple black bra.

That was when I froze.

It wasn't like I'd never done this before. Christ, I'd been messing around with girls a hell of a lot earlier than most boys should. Gina was just one of too many who seemed to like a bad boy in their bed, and before her, I'd been a bona fide expert at using rickety fire escapes to avoid angry parents after I'd defiled their daughters in the next room.

But this was different.

I wanted Lea. I wanted her more than I had ever wanted anyone.

But as I took in her perfect skin, those hopeful eyes, and her beautiful body splayed out before me like a buffet waiting to be sampled, only one thing echoed through my head.

She deserves better.

So I pushed myself up. "No." My voice was hoarse with want, but I said it again anyway. "No, Lea. I'm sorry, baby. We have to stop."

FIFTEEN

WAY PAST TURNING BACK

Lea

"Are you *fucking* kidding me?"

Michael blinked. And I practically flew off the couch.

Shame. Two seconds ago, I had been hotter than a tea kettle and about ready to whistle, but now I only wanted to cover myself back up. This man had been all over me, and for the first time, I was ready, really ready, to lay myself bare for another person. Literally.

And as soon as I did, he didn't want it.

"Shit. Fuck. Lea, Tess, don't cry. Baby, please."

"Don't baby me, you asshole," I snapped through the tears that were already welling up despite my best efforts to stop them. Somehow, my shirt had lost its opening. And sleeves. "And don't use that stupid fucking nickname, either. My name is not Tess!"

Before I even managed to pull my shirt back over my head again, his arms were around me, pulling me back against his broad, warm chest. His breath was warm against my ear as he shushed away my tears.

It only made me fall apart more.

Gently, he turned me around, cocooning me with his body while he rocked me back and forth. One hand threaded into my hair as he cradled my head against his chest, the other wrapped securely about my waist.

"Don't you get it?" His deep voice quavered. "I'm not stopping because I don't want you, Lea. I'm stopping because I want you too fuckin' much. I'm stopping because I know if I give in to this, I won't be able to stop."

His hand tightened in my hair, and I could practically feel the desperation vibrating through him. Fear and need flickered in his deep brown eyes, along with a fire that threatened to burn me alive if I let it.

I should have followed his lead. Let him call it off, run out of that room. Gone back to the life where I was the good girl, the older sister, the one everyone trusted but no one really loved.

Not all the way.

Not like this.

The thought made the tears threaten to spill over. I hadn't even realized that's how I felt until I was here with this man, in his arms, absorbing warmth, adoration, and what it meant to be truly desired for the first time in my life.

It was even more dangerous considering that I wanted him like that too.

This wasn't me shucking my V-card at a party to catch up with my friends and sister. This was real. It *meant* something.

But apparently, it didn't go both ways.

I swallowed hard. "Then why are you talking to me like a lover if you don't want me that way?" My voice was barely above a choked whisper.

Michael exhaled a long breath, and his body relaxed slightly. "Because every time I'm with you, I feel alive, like maybe I've never been before. Not in this shitty life I've lived. But I also feel like I'm living on borrowed time. I don't want to give you up, Lea. I can't. But I also can't give in and risk losing everything neither."

His words hung, netted in a strange mixture of anger and longing. I wanted to slap him for his confusion, for his weakness, but I also wanted to pull him closer and let him know that I understood.

"Why?" I murmured. "What would you lose?"

He shook his head. And really, I didn't need him to answer. I practically shouted that I was an adult, but I lived with his boss. He hadn't explicitly said that Nonno had made me and my sisters off-limits to his employees, but I couldn't imagine that my old-school grandpa would ever want any of them, much less one with a record getting into bed with his granddaughter.

Just the idea of his reaction put the fear of God in me. And considering that all Michael had right now was this breakroom and Nonno's good graces, he had a lot more to lose if we were caught.

"You don't need to say it," I whispered into his chest, my voice barely audible. "I get it. We both know that we're playing with fire."

He pulled me closer until our lips were almost touching. "You have no idea," he growled, his eyes burning into mine. "No fuckin' clue."

We stared at each other for a long time. Past the point where my tears had dried. The hand in my hair tightened so that a bite of pain threaded through his deft touch. I didn't hate it. I didn't hate it at all.

Especially when Michael's gaze dropped to my lips and stayed there.

"Fuck, Lea…" he drifted off. "If we start again…I don't think I can stop myself."

Which meant I should stop him. His meaning was clear—he was losing his self-control, but he would follow mine.

Unfortunately, that had skipped out the door with the rest of my self-respect.

"Then don't," I said as I pulled him close. "*Please, don't stop.*"

One moment, Michael's hands were threaded in my hair, his body a wall against mine, and the next, our lips were locked in another searing kiss. It was as if all the tension and unspoken emotions from the evening had been distilled into this one perfect moment.

His mouth was rough, his kiss fierce and passionate, as if everything he'd been holding back inside him had finally found an escape. The walls of the room seemed to dissolve, and the air around us grew thick with emotion. His hands slid down my back, pulling me closer, deeper into the embrace, sliding down to take solid handfuls of my ass in a way that told me that this time he wasn't letting go for anything.

Michael hadn't been kidding when he said he wanted me too much to stop. It was as if every ounce of desire he contained had been unleashed. His hands explored me, pulling my shirt out of my hands, tugging at my pants, and then pulling them and my boots off until I stood before him in nothing but my bra and panties.

It was the most naked I'd ever been with a boy. With anyone, really.

"Are you sure about this?" he asked, as his fingertips played up and down my spine, quivering with anticipation. I could hear the tremor in his voice, the uncertainty that, despite his rock-solid exterior, he felt too.

But this wasn't laced with guilt. It was more like awe. That, like me, he couldn't quite believe this was really happening. That it could ever feel so good.

I took a deep breath, then another, before I finally nodded. "Yes," I whispered. "I'm sure."

He smiled a little, his eyes dark and hungry. Then he pulled me back against him, his lips meeting mine again.

A wave of anticipation raced through me. With one swift movement, his hands moved to my waist, pulling me flush against his solid form. His unmistakable hardness pressed into my belly through his jeans, teasing a heart-wrenching gasp. Those talented fingers began at the curve of my hipbone, gliding across my panties, then tracing the contour of my body with a familiarity that spoke volumes of his desires. Each touch lighter than a feather but turned my insides molten.

"Are you wet?" he whispered huskily against my earlobe, nipping it softly before trailing kisses down my neck.

The question made me whimper; it was so raw and primal. Neither polite nor gentle. Open desire expressed in words.

"Yes," I barely managed to exhale.

"Let's see, then."

Two skilled fingers slipped under the delicate fabric of my underwear and brushed over that most sensitive place. I bit back a moan.

Deftly, he began to explore. Finding the sensitive skin of my inner thighs, toying with the elastic edges of my underwear, stroking underneath every so often. I arched against him, shaking from nerves and desire alike.

I didn't know how to tell him the truth. That despite my talk, this was the farthest I'd ever gone. That Victor had slipped a hand under my skirt while we were watching *Top Gun*, but I'd jumped up from the couch as soon as I heard Nonna's keys in the front door. Two weeks later, he was in Gina Reyes's arms. And since then, there had been no one. Stolen kisses at school dances and catcalls on the street did not experience make.

I wanted more, but I was barely aware of what *more* was. It was basically all theory at this point.

Michael's touch, however, was extremely real.

"This all right?" Michael asked as I writhed against his exploring fingers.

"I–I don't—oh!"

His thumb dipped lower circled around the slick bundle of nerves I only touched in the shower or on the few occasions I had my bedroom to myself. It was so much—almost too much.

Michael seemed to understand. He withdrew his hand, then tugged me back onto the couch with him so I was straddling his lap.

"Come here," he murmured as he threaded one hand back into my hair to pull me down for another kiss.

It was like he understood that his mouth soothed me as much as it made me come alive. That kiss didn't just light a fire but also unlocked something deep inside me. Someplace that felt like home.

I wanted *more* again. And if the erection pulsing under his jeans was any indication, so did he.

"Lea," Michael sputtered as I rolled my hips toward him. "I—"

"Hush," I said, pulling him back to me, grinding onto him again. I was acting out of instinct, without any real awareness of what I was doing.

Well, it seemed to be working for him. It certainly was for me.

"Jesus." His hands, large and capable, slipped up my side to cup my breasts, thumbs playing over my nipples.

I shuddered as he pulled down the elastic cups. I wasn't particularly large, but my nipples were sensitive. Even more so when he drew one into his mouth with a heavy sigh and worshiped the tip with his tongue.

"Michael." It was the only word I could say as I pulled his head closer, urging him on.

He switched to my other breast while his hands fell back to my ass, taking lush handfuls of flesh to knead like pastry. I rolled into each movement as he suckled; I moaned and bit his ear. His growl was long and low before he release my nipple with a pop.

"Jesus, Lea," he said again. "Slow down, baby. You're gonna make me—"

"Come?" I smiled against his mouth when he tilted his head up for another kiss. "Eventually, maybe."

He growled again against my neck. "Definitely."

A thrill ran up my spine as he scattered kisses all over my chest, then went back to his work on my breast. My body was thrown into a frenzy as his fingertips brushed my center through my underwear, teasing the wet heat there that throbbed for him. He wanted me. He wanted me bad. This was about to happen, really happen.

Holy shit.

"More," I mumbled, sliding my hands under his shirt and touching the muscles that flexed under my fingertips.

"Take it," he said, then pulled his shirt over his head, revealing the broad, tattooed expanse of his muscled chest and the heavy cross on a silver chain that swung over his sternum. "Take whatever you fuckin' want, Tess. It all belongs to you anyway."

"I…" I stared at him. At the winding tattoos that swirled over his pecs and abs and even up one side of his neck. At the muscles that flexed and pulled under my touch. At the eager gleam in his eye that was expecting…something.

Something I wanted. But something I had no idea how to get it.

"I—I don't know what to do," I blurted out, then immediately flushed with embarrassment.

I didn't like feeling incompetent. I was smart, and I had listened to my friends. Even if I didn't have much experience, I should know this. It was supposed to come naturally. Right?

Gently, two fingers under my chin rotated my face back to his.

"Baby." His brown eyes were warm as they looked me over. "Lea. You're a…shit, you're a virgin."

My face bloomed with heat. "Did you think I forgot?"

I couldn't help the edge of my tone. I didn't want to be defensive, but what if he didn't want me anymore after remembering that choice bit of information? Even worse, what if he'd heard about me before? What if he knew about Cherry Popper, that stupid name, that stupid reputation that went along with it?

Michael let out a small laugh, his eyes softening. "*I* almost did. That's what you do to me."

I bit my lip, suddenly uneasy. "Is it a problem?"

The hands on my thighs gave them a friendly squeeze. "No, Tess. It's not a problem."

"Really?" I squeaked.

He chuckled again, then stroked my face. "No. But maybe we'll…take our time."

I frowned. "You want to stop?"

He cocked his head. "Do you?"

Immediately, I shook my head. "No. This feels good. I just want to keep feeling good."

Michael pulled me close for another deep, mind-altering kiss. "I think I can handle that."

He continued kissing me as his hand played with the elastic of my underwear, then eventually pulled it aside.

"Tell me if you want me to stop," he said as his thumb drifted up and down my core.

I shuddered as it found my clit. "I won't."

There was another chuckle, replaced by a voracious

kiss as his fingers traveled lower, and then one slipped inside me and started a slow rhythm that quickly rendered me breathless and clinging to him for support.

"You like that?" His voice rumbled against my ear, and his breathing was heavy, but it felt like an honest question.

"I—oh! Yesss," I hissed as he nibbled on my ear.

My body arched into his touch, my breath growing more ragged and desperate. His fingers moved inside me, exploring and teasing until my body was writhing against his. Bliss took me over, rendering me unable to think of anything except the unbearable anticipation and the exquisite ache that throbbed deep inside me.

He knew what I wanted, and he was giving it to me, little by little. I clung to him desperately, my breaths coming in short, ragged gulps and my heart pounding wildly in my chest.

As his fingers worked their magic, Michael kissed me again. A second finger joined the first, stretching me and sending me into a frenzy of pleasure and need. His fingers were familiar and yet foreign, even more as his thumb settled over my clit and found a rhythm to match the other two.

"Are you ready?" he asked, his voice a low growl. His breath was hot and heavy against my skin.

"Y-yes," I whimpered. Though for what, I wasn't sure.

I knew what orgasms felt like, at least when I gave them to myself. But the anticipation had never felt like this. Not with this dripping, anxious, body-wrenching desire to be close, closer, closer, without any understanding of how it could happen. It was like comparing a drizzle to a rainstorm. Didn't even come close.

As my mind reeled and my body braced itself against the oncoming tidal wave, Michael's knowing hand continued to expertly move within me. I was dizzy with want, barely able to register the feel of his lips on my neck, my ear, even tugging my breast between his teeth. I knew what I wanted, what my body craved, but I had never had anyone guide me through it before. I had never trusted anyone enough to let them in, to let them take control.

But now, Michael was showing me how. He was teaching me to let go in ways my body understood, in ways my mind couldn't comprehend. I was putty in his hands, falling, tumbling headlong into a world of pleasure. Terrifying but thrilling all at once.

His fingers continued to tease and stroke, and I knew I was close.

"That's it, my contessa," he rumbled. "Fuck my hand, baby. Let me feel you come."

And so, I did. The wave within me broke, and I surrendered completely to its ebb and flow, to the raw, animalistic need that was coursing through me with the strength of a riptide.

"Michael!" The cry choked me, but he covered it with kisses, swallowing the rest of my shouts as I came undone on his lap.

I shuddered and gasped for air, my body still shaking even as he slipped his fingers from my depths, leaving my core throbbing and sensitive. His chest welcomed my collapse while his other hand played up and down my spine, and his heartbeat thumped solidly under my cheek.

Eventually, I returned to the moment. To this room that I had made for us, in a way. It offered a bit of peace, knowing that.

But while my body was languid and loose from my release, his was anything but. Especially the part of him that was still encased in denim and hard as stone between my thighs.

Somehow, I managed to push myself up.

His brown eyes were big and searching when they found mine.

"You're so fucking beautiful," he whispered as his hands drew a path over my back. "You all right?"

I nodded. "I'm good. But what about, um, you?"

I looked down and, seized with a bit of bravery, set my hand on his erection. It actually moved at my touch.

Michael jerked. "Fuck."

I giggled, unable to help myself. "It's like it's saying hello."

With a dry look, he moved my hand away.

"I—why?" I found myself asking as he pulled it back to his chest.

Shame flickered through my bliss once more. Was something wrong? Didn't he want me too?

"Because," he murmured as he continued caressing my back with his other hand, "you deserve better than a quickie in a breakroom for your first time, Tess. You deserve a hell of a lot more than I can give you—"

"Don't start that again," I cut in, pushing back up. "You can't leave me alone after that, Michael Scarrone. I won't let you."

To my surprise, I received no argument—just a perfectly beautiful boyish grin.

"Oh, I won't argue," he said before kissing me again. "We're in this now, baby. You got me hooked. You'll never get rid of me, I'm sorry to say."

My insides practically glowed. "I'm okay with that."

"I only meant that we don't have to rush," Michael continued. "We can take our time. Make sure you're ready."

I tipped my head with a shy smile. "So I get more than the one date now?"

Michael's big hands clasped my face, pulling me down for one final kiss. "I sure as shit hope so, Tess. I'll take as many as I can get."

SIXTEEN

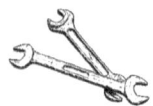

STORIES ETCHED IN INK AND HEARTBREAK

Michael

"What does this tattoo mean?" Lea asked some time later.

I chuckled as I stroked her hair. She lay on my bare chest, still recovering her breath after yelling my name through three more orgasms, exploring the various tattoos that littered my body.

I looked down to where she was pointing at the skull and crossbones on my ribs.

I made a face. "That one is so fuckin' whack. What am I, a pirate? I got it when I was maybe fifteen because I thought it was cool. Probably have it covered with something else when I have the money."

Lea chuckled, probably because I'd given her similar responses for every tattoo she'd asked about so far. My hips arched automatically as her fingers danced down my abs, playing above my belt buckle. She'd offered a few times to undo it, to give me some of the pleasure I'd been providing her for the last few hours.

But I'd stopped her every time. Not because I didn't want it—fuck me, did I want it. I probably wanted it more than any man on the planet had ever wanted it.

I was starting to realize that something about Lea made me feel a little old-fashioned. I didn't want our first time—and at this point, I'd bet my life there would actually *be* a first time—to be a transaction. I wanted it to be special. I wanted it to be good enough for someone like her.

Which how I found myself repeatedly turning down *that* particular offer for the first time ever.

"Did you get all of them because they're cool?" she teased as I placed a hand over hers, stilling its progress across my chest.

Typically, I said "yes" when people asked me some version of that question. I'd even been in a situation almost like this with my last girlfriend—with Gina— when, in the blissful dream right after sex, she'd some- times pepper me with personal questions. Like she knew that was the best time to ask them, that it was maybe the only time I would actually answer her.

But Lea didn't know that. Probably because she already knew I'd answer her questions at any time of day.

I was already an open book with her.

It was dangerous. But I couldn't bring myself to care.

"No," I said honestly. "Not all of them."

Her finger drifted over my chest, leaving a trail of goose bumps in its wake. "Which ones are important?"

I didn't answer for a long time. I focused on the water stain in the plaster above the bed, then on the portrait of St. Christopher hanging over the little table and chair set. Lea remained quiet. So much more patient than usual.

Apparently, that was the effect of even a little bit of sex on my girl. I wondered what the real thing would do.

Eventually, though, I pointed to a spot on my upper pec, to the left of my sternum. I didn't have to look at where I was pointing. I knew exactly where this bit of ink was.

Lea pushed up off my chest so she could hover over me, her dark hair a silky sheet over one shoulder that tickled my arm as she examined the cursive name on my left pec. It was surrounded by a wreath of wings and a halo inked in gold lines.

"Tommy," she read. "Who's that?"

I swallowed and remained focused on the St. Christopher picture, where the saint's head was surrounded by a similarly drawn halo. "He was my little brother."

Lea looked up, green eyes bright with surprise. "You had a brother? I didn't know you had any family."

I shook my head. "I don't. Not anymore." I swallowed hard. "It's, ah, hard to talk about."

Her expression managed to be sympathetic without pity. I had to give it to her; it was a hard combination.

"Yeah," she said quietly. "I understand that."

She did, I realized. And she had still told me her story on the train.

I figured I could at least repay the favor.

"He was six years younger than me," I told her. "Different dads, though. He, um, was in foster care for a long time after my mom took off."

"Why did she leave?"

"She..." I never knew how to answer that question. "I don't really know," I said honestly. "Drugs, probably. She got sucked into crack in the eighties, I think. When Tommy was about a year old, she dumped us at her sister-in-law's place, and we never saw her again. I heard she OD'd when I was maybe fourteen, but I could never track her down completely."

"Where was your dad?"

"He's serving time upstate. Forty years for two counts of murder."

I could have told her the gritty details, but I trusted she could fill in the blanks. My dad wasn't a good guy— never had been, never would be.

"Anyway," I said. "Tommy's dad was a one-night stand. He never even acknowledged him."

She didn't ask why my mom had never sued for paternity or anything like that. We both knew that, even if she had wanted it, the cost of court, lawyers, all that would have stopped her. Just like it did so many others.

"The thing was, Tommy had cerebral palsy. And my mom couldn't deal. He wasn't—he needed other—" I broke off, shaking my head. "I couldn't take care of him by myself. Not the way he needed."

"Well, of course you couldn't. You were only a kid." Lea's matter-of-factness pulled me out of the haze of shame that always clouded my head whenever I thought about Tommy.

"You did," I said evenly. "You and your brother took care of your sisters."

"Doesn't mean we did a good job," she replied just as evenly. "And it doesn't mean we should have had to, either."

We were quiet for a minute while she let that set in. Eventually, I relaxed the fists I hadn't realized I'd made and kept talking, fully aware that if I didn't finish this story, she'd get it out of me anyway.

Which might have been exactly what I needed.

"He lived in this group home that specialized in helping kids like him," I said. "Kids with special needs. I was moved around a lot until I was in high school. Then I ran off for good. Bounced around sleeping on friends' couches, things like that. You know the rest. But I...I always checked on Tommy. Made sure they were treating him all right."

"Were they?" Lea asked. She seemed more afraid of that answer than of the others I'd offered.

I shrugged. "Best they could, I think. But cerebral palsy can have a lot of complications. Sometimes, with the way the body grows, things don't come up until later. Four years ago, Tommy started having really bad seizures. Like sometimes they would stop his heart."

Her hand pressed to her heart as if in response. "Oh, shit."

"Yeah. He was on meds, but he needed this risky surgery to fix the problem. But the state insurance wouldn't cover it until he'd tried all the meds he could."

She sucked in a breath. "So it wasn't for Paul Reyes. Stealing the cars, I mean."

Damn, she was quick. Had a mind like a damn calculator.

"No," I admitted. "He did have a debt—I didn't lie about that—but it wasn't that big. The Mancusos offered to front me the money for Tommy's surgery if I finished the other jobs."

I didn't need to fill in the rest.

"So…did he? Did he get the surgery, at least?"

Feeling like my tongue was tied into a knot, I shook my head, pointed to the date on my chest, and stared back up at the ceiling again.

"September sixteenth, two thousand," Lea read. Her voice warbled a little. "He died?"

I squeezed my eyes shut. "One of his seizures stopped his heart. While I was stuck in Rikers."

When I finally had the courage to open my eyes again, a tear slipped down my cheek. I couldn't fucking help it. I tried not to talk about Tommy, and this here was exactly the reason why.

"Better you know now what you're getting," I said quietly. "That's what I got running through my veins, Tess. A father who murders. An addict mother who abandons. And I'm already following in their footsteps. A thief with a record. No fuckin' good."

Before I was even finished, Lea had gripped my chin and forced me to turn my head toward her. I almost shut my eyes again to avoid that arrow-tipped gaze. Fuck, she really could see right through me.

But she was so brave. She was taking me on when the whole world told her not to. Let me spill my secrets. Give her the heart of what I really was, ugly though it might be.

I could at least listen to whatever she had to say in return.

So I looked back, and that was when I saw tears that mirrored my own, creating a bright sheen over a green gaze that was as direct as ever.

As strong as ever.

As *mine* as ever.

"People are so much more than their parents, Michael," she said solemnly.

I blinked. "You—do you really believe that?"

"Absolutely." Her voice was low but fierce. "I'm proof of it. And so are you."

We stared at each other for a long time, two broken souls somehow melding into one.

I didn't believe in miracles until that exact moment.

Until she taught me how.

She held my gaze until my breathing returned to normal. Until the tattoo on my chest didn't feel like it was burning anymore, and my heart rate dropped to its slow, regular rhythm.

"Come here," I said roughly, pulling her back down to me.

I kissed her harder than I intended, then rolled her onto her back and kissed her some more.

"Michael," she whispered again and again as I started to make my way down her body. Her fingers threaded into my hair. "My Michael."

I could only hum in agreement. What else could I do? The only other option was to acknowledge the way her few questions, her no-nonsense manner, and her beautifully open face were ripping down every fence I'd been hiding behind since I was barely able to walk. Declare that, for better or for worse, I was, in fact, her Michael now. In all honesty, I probably had been from the beginning.

SEVENTEEN

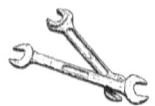

NO, YOU HANG UP FIRST, BUT WITHOUT A PHONE

Michael

"I'm not leaving until you go."

I smiled against Lea's lips, then sucked on the bottom one again for good measure before shaking my head. "Go on, baby girl. You need to get inside before your grandparents wonder where you are."

She kissed me again, and this time, I was tempted to take her back to the garage and start Part Two of Ruining Lea Zola's Innocence.

But when a light on the top floor of her house switched on, I managed to pull away.

"Lea," I said, my voice rough with need. "Fuck. Baby, we gotta stop."

She smirked, hands wrapped around my waist. "Please. You don't want me to stop."

"I definitely don't," I admitted while she did something to my neck that almost made me drag her down the alley to hide in the shadows like the thief I was.

"But I'm also not interested in my boss popping his head out while I cop a feel of his granddaughter. And since I'm not leaving until I know you're inside, safe and warm, you need to go in first."

She giggled, then bit my ear.

I groaned. "Lea, Jesus."

"Relax, I'm going. But I thought of something."

The hopeful look on her face erased my worries. I wonder if she already knew she had this effect on me. That a little honey caught me like a damn fly, and I'd probably do whatever she wanted if she looked at me like that.

"I thought maybe you'd want to come over tomorrow," she said. "I'll make us some dinner, and we could watch a movie, hang out."

She pulled mischievously on the collar of my jacket, urging me to kiss her again. And I wanted to. I really did. Just like I wanted to do all those things she was suggesting. They were so simple. Basic shit that kids our age did every weekend. Things I hadn't done in years.

I glanced up at the front window of her house. No one was there, but that didn't mean they couldn't be in a second. "I don't think so, Tess. It's not a good idea."

That hopeful expression disappeared, and it was like a punch to the gut. Lea looked me over like she was trying to find some missing piece to the puzzle. Then she glanced at the window and back to me with understanding written all over her pretty face.

"I'm not an idiot," she told me. "I know you're not supposed to get involved with me."

I frowned. "You do?"

"Sure. Nonno's been telling all his mechanics to

steer clear since I was probably twelve. He's a bit over-protective."

Something inside me thawed. I knew it probably meant nothing, but the fact that Zola hadn't singled me out with that warning felt, I don't know, kind of good. Like maybe he didn't only think of me as a no-good kid. Like maybe this job—and by extension, this girl—really was a second chance.

It also meant that there was even more pressure not to fuck it up. We didn't need to rush into anything. Even though I already knew I was pretty much a goner, there was no guarantee Lea felt the same way. We could take our time. See how things went. I'd try to learn how to be an asset to her family, not dead weight. I'd make them see that having me around would be a blessing, not a curse.

How, I had no idea. But for the first time in my life, it really felt possible.

"They just have to get used to the idea," she continued. "You're a good person, Michael. Nonno knows that. He wouldn't have hired you otherwise."

I wanted to believe her. I really did. But something told me that my grizzled old boss wasn't quite open-minded enough to accept an ex-con dating his grand-daughter. Not any time soon, at least.

"But they wouldn't be here anyway."

"They won't?"

Lea shook her head. "Joni has a dance show in Philly tomorrow night. They're taking my sisters and staying with Nonno's brother. Won't be back until Mass."

Well, that got my attention.

"How come you're not going?" I couldn't imagine the Zolas letting Lea get out of the recital because she didn't feel like it.

Lea shrugged. "I have to study for a biology exam and work on some more scholarship applications. But I can't study all night…"

Envy twisted through my gut at the thought of Lea's family life. Her sisters, her grandparents, and her home all seemed so perfect the way they supported her and actively wanted her to do things like go to college and reach her goals. I hadn't even considered things like the SATs or scholarships when I was in high school. When other kids were thinking about college, I was too busy running around the streets with my friends, dreaming about cars and girls.

Lea had a family. A future. She didn't even know how lucky that made her.

I just wanted to be a part of it.

"You sure?" I asked, even as my hands slipped around her waist again.

She grinned. "Absolutely. Study breaks are good for the brain."

I chuckled. I wasn't exactly planning breaks that would make her think straight.

"Fine." I gave in, unable to resist. "What time?"

Lea's eyes lit up, and she threw her arms around me, pulling my head down for another kiss. "Seven," she said before releasing me at last and turning to walk up the steps to her house. "In time for diner. And don't be late, Mr. Scarrone."

"Wouldn't dream of it, contessa."

I waited until the front door had shut behind her, then turned back toward the garage.

I'd barely taken three steps when two men emerged from the park across the street.

"Yo, Mikey."

Paul Reyes crossed the street diagonally, accompanied by another dude wearing an oversized black parka. He yanked at his sagging pants while he walked, as if they would fall down otherwise.

"Fuck," I muttered, then continued on my way.

They caught up to me quickly, each one falling into step on either side of me as we crossed into the shadows, away from the busy part of Belmont.

"Don't run off, now," Paul said with a grin that revealed one of his gold teeth. "We're just being friendly."

"Not as friendly as he was with Lea Zola," snarked the other one. "Tryin' to fuck the Cherry Popper, huh? Maybe she'll finally give it up for him."

In a flash, I had the guy up against the wall. He was a slimy little worm, short enough then with my arm under his neck, he had to pop up onto his toes to keep from choking.

"You will keep that name outta your motherfuckin' mouth," I said quietly, but directly into the guy's ear so he had no choice but to listen. "Who's the joker, Paulie? He's got a lot to say for someone with shit for brains."

"Chill, man, chill." Paul chuckled, like I didn't have his friend pinned against the bricks. "This is Jay. He don't mean nothing. He's a new runner I'm training. For Antoni and Mancuso."

Even gasping for breath, Jay managed to smirk.

He knew the power of Paul's pronouncement. He knew I was going to let him go because of those names.

I hated myself a little for it, but I did.

He wheezed and collapsed against the wall when I released him.

I turned to Paul. "What do you want?"

"I can't check on my old friend Mikey?"

"It's Michael," I said, surprising even myself. "Or Mike. And we're not friends. Even when I was with Gina."

A black cloud shadowed Paul's face at the mention of his sister. "Yeah, she ain't gonna be happy to hear about what I saw tonight, neither. Since when have you been hooking up with the frigid Zola sister?"

"Since never," I lied, praying they'd only caught the end of the interaction. "She's my boss's granddaughter. I was walking her home."

"Well, aren't you the fuckin' gentleman." Jay danced out of my reach as he spoke. "Nobody is that familiar with girls they're 'walkin' home."

I ignored him and waited for Paul to get to the point. He wanted something. That much was clear.

"Sly Ricky wants you to drive to Newark tomorrow night."

I scowled. "With what car? I told you, I'm not driving. Repair only."

"You have access," Paul countered. "I saw you take a Chevelle out on Tuesday."

"That was to test the engine," I said. "I don't fuckin' drive."

"Yeah, but he ain't gonna be around tomorrow," Jay

put in after he stood up and took several steps out of my reach.

"The girl told you," Paul agreed. "She told the whole neighborhood."

"And nothing's going to happen," I snapped. "You didn't hear anything."

"I heard something," Jay said, still out of reach. "I heard plenty."

"Mike."

Paul's eyes had gone hard. The jokes were over. It was time to get down to business.

"I gave you time," he said. "What, a few weeks? But it's time you did what's right. Sly Ricky already asked for your help with a job. He ain't gonna ask again."

"Or what?" I sneered. "You gonna pull another knife on me, Paulie? You want me to tell you what I'd do if you tried that shit on me again?"

The smaller man shuddered slightly, as if he knew good and well what I was capable of. He'd caught me by surprise once. It wasn't going to happen again. Hand to hand, I could take them. I had at least fifty pounds on Paulie, probably twenty on his buddy.

To my surprise, Paul relaxed, as if he had realized he wasn't getting anywhere with me this way.

"I tell you what," Paul said. "Show up tomorrow, and we don't tell old man Zola that you're tryna get with his granddaughter. And my sister don't need to know nothing either."

I narrowed my eyes at him, then glanced to my left, where his friend huffed at my shoulders.

"I'll show up," I said. "But only to tell Ricky to his face that I'm out, whether he likes it or not."

I walked away without looking back. It was one of the biggest flexes you could make in this neighborhood. Turning your back on a man in the dark meant you weren't afraid.

And I sure as shit wasn't afraid of Paul Reyes or that weasel he called a friend.

Unfortunately, that was my biggest mistake.

Five seconds later, I was shoved against the wall, the combined body weight of Paul and Jay enough to keep me there while Paul pulled up his shirt to reveal that he was carrying a lot more than a knife this time.

"On second thought," he said. "Ricky wanted to see you tonight. And the way I'm feeling, I'm going to enjoy watching you squirm when you finally get what's coming to you."

EIGHTEEN

NEVER SKIP OUT ON A MOBSTER

Michael

Twenty minutes later, I was hustled out of the back of Paul Reyes's Yukon and up the stairs of a nondescript brick building in Morrisania. It was the kind of place where the numbers were always ripped off no matter how many times the city replaced them. No one wanted the police or EMTs or anyone poking around here. Addresses were for traceable suckers.

But I'd always recognize the heart of the operation that ruined me.

"I got it," I snapped when Paul nearly tripped me while shoving me through a door on the third floor. "I can walk, you fuckin' parasite."

"Paul. Jay. There's no need to be uncivilized with our guest."

A deep voice with a thick Eastern European accent commanded the room in a second. Paul and Jay released their grips, and I shook them off like a dog right out of water. I then took an extra second to straighten my clothes before peering around a room I'd thought I'd never see again.

It wasn't really a room—more like four hollowed-out apartments that once upon a time took up half the third floor. Weight-bearing posts were scattered around the room, along with a few remnants of the apartments that used to be here—a kitchen in one corner, a full bar built in another, a TV surrounded by couches near an empty fireplace, and a large dining table that would easily seat ten or twelve and chairs set up in the middle. There were a few other tables here and there that were currently empty, but I could easily imagine holding a card game or two.

The headquarters of the Mancuso family was big but not particularly showy. Made sense. Most of the bosses didn't even live in the Bronx anymore. Instead, they made their homes in Westchester and New Jersey, leaving the dirty work of managing their turf to low-level soldiers or runners like Paul and Jay.

They were blasé about my presence—no blindfolds or passwords or dumb movie shit like that. That was because they knew, just as I did, that there wouldn't be a single incriminating piece of evidence in the building. Mobsters like Mancuso and Antoni provided the money and the protection for various operations like selling dope, stealing cars, or gambling, and in exchange, they took a healthy cut. But none of it ever touched them because they were smart and played men like me for fools. It was why they were so hard to take down. And why it was so hard to escape them.

No, a place like this had two purposes: congregation and interrogation.

I doubted I was here for the first.

The merging of the Albanians and the Italians had been coming a long time in Belmont. The Albanians had been steadily taking over the drug trade in this part of the city since the early eighties, doing the work no one else wanted to do with ruthlessness, efficiency, and immovable integrity. They kept their promises unto death—or so said their reputation. It made them valuable partners. And certainly not people you'd ever want to cross.

This was the first time I'd met any of them, though.

"Sit," said the man who was clearly in charge. He gestured to a seat at the far end of the dining table.

Not being a complete idiot, I did what he said.

Five men sat with him, some sipping on espresso or glasses of brown liquid, others picking at a platter of baklava, while a few others were watching a Knicks game on the TV, and a blonde woman in the kitchen was busy at the counter. At the head of the table was a middle-aged guy with thinning gray hair and a long, slightly crooked nose. Everyone else, including Sly Ricky, was watching him closely.

But it was the familiar face sitting to his right that clued me in to the fact that I was facing none other than Lis Antoni, boss of the entire Albanian mafia in New York City.

"Ares." I nodded to my former classmate. "What up, man?"

I hadn't seen Ares Antoni since the ninth grade,

which happened to be both of our last years of high school. Our reasons, however, were pretty damn different. I left because no one cared whether I passed or failed. Ares left because people cared too much. His life had already been planned for him by the people in this room, and those plans didn't require Algebra Two or reading *Huckleberry Finn*.

I had to give it to Lis Antoni. It was a pretty strong declaration to name your only son after the god of fucking war.

"Hey," Ares replied with a simple nod. He'd grown up since ninth grade, switched the oversized Knicks jersey for a button-up shirt, a buzz-cut for slicked brown hair, and a babyface for a well-groomed goatee.

Still as quiet as ever, though. It made sense. A god of war in training was never going to waste time with chatter.

The woman in the kitchen approached the table, carrying a tray of food, which she set down directly next to Ares. He gave me a smirk when he saw that I recognized her.

Gina Reyes. Paul's sister and my ex-girlfriend.

Apparently, she wasn't too eager to get me back as everyone thought. Not that I gave a shit.

Although I was a little surprised that Area was into her now. Fine as she was, I wouldn't have thought he'd have a taste for sloppy seconds.

"You want?" Lis's deep voice boomed across the table as he waved a casual hand toward the food.

I shook my head. "I'm good, thanks."

"Hi, Mike." Gina finished unloading the tray, giving

everyone at the table an ample look at her cleavage in the process. But instead of turning to Ares, she slid a proprietary arm around Lis's shoulder on her other side.

No one at the table even batted an eye.

"How you been, baby?" she purred as she played with the older man's hair.

I shouldn't have been surprised. Gina always did have a taste for power and the darker corners of Belmont, even if it only started with star basketball players and hoods like me. But the sight of her hand massaging the neck of a dude at least forty years older than her was still pretty fucked up.

"I heard you got out," she continued as she massaged Lis's neck.

"Yes, no thanks to you," I snapped before I could stop myself.

I'd asked Gina to write a letter to the judge on my behalf, hoping I could manage probation instead of prison time. She hadn't come through despite being the only one I could turn to back then. The judge had taken one look at me, wished out loud he had the power of mandatory minimums, and slapped me with a two-year sentence with no time off for good behavior.

It was as if my bitterness poisoned the whole room.

"Leave us," Lis told Gina as he removed her arm from his shoulder.

He didn't even look at her, and neither did anyone else, not even her brother. Judging by the gold hanging from her neck and ears, I had a feeling Lis was paying for the privilege of obedience in every way possible. Gina could play mob wife all she wanted, but it was obvious to everyone that she wasn't nothing but a cheap side piece.

I chuckled. Gina's eyes flamed.

She opened her mouth as if to snap at me, but the older man's expression shut her mouth.

Even so, she waved at me on her way out. Every other man in the room watched as she sauntered away, swaying her hips in that way I knew very well.

I didn't watch, though. It was like trying to go back to day-old burgers after you'd tasted a good steak for the very first time.

The door closed behind her, and I faced the group, which felt weirdly like déjà vu. It was always going to come to this, I realized. I had to stand before the parole board to get out of Rikers. Now I had to stand before these guys to be free in my own damn neighborhood.

"Michael Scarrone," said Lis after he took a sip of his espresso. "You're a hard man to track down."

"Don't know why," I replied. "I've been working since I got out, but not hiding anywhere. I'm straight now and good with that."

"He don't listen," Paul spat beside me. He had not, I noticed, been asked to sit down. "Arrogant prick thinks he's too good to come and pay his respect—"

"That's enough," Lis snapped. "A man should speak for himself." He turned back to me. "You were asked to come to a meeting with Riccardo and my partner. You did not. Why?"

I managed to stop glaring at Paul long enough to answer Lis's question. "I didn't see a reason to come."

"The invitation wasn't enough? It's rude to ignore."

Ricky snickered. I shot him a glare, then looked

back at Lis. I had a fine line to walk here. A boss like him loved nothing more than to make an example. But he wouldn't respect a pussy, either.

"I kept my promise to Mancuso," I said. "Brought in the cars he needed. Served my time when I was caught. Kept my trap shut."

Lis nodded. "It's true. You did. This was admirable."

The other Albanians in the room grumbled their agreement.

"Well, good," I said. "So we're square, Mancuso and me."

We weren't square. I'd never be square with these crooked fucks. Would have served them right if I'd snitched on them too, seeing as they'd cost me my brother. My whole fuckin' life.

I didn't owe Sly Ricky, Bertie Mancuso, or Lis Antoni one raw cent.

"Yes," Lis began, and I was already looking toward the door when he said one last word that spilled the end. "Except."

Dread draped around my shoulders like a cape. "Yeah?"

He glanced around the table. "Problem is…what's the problem, Riccardo?"

Sly Ricky offered a grin, one that showed a gold tooth in the back of his mouth and probably earned him his nickname. "He knows too much."

"He knows too much," repeated Lis like a grade school teacher parroting their students.

"I don't know anything," I insisted. "And that's what

I'll always say. I kept my end of the bargain, even after Ricky here welched on our deal."

"I didn't welch on nothin'!" Ricky sputtered, red-faced, when Lis pivoted that sharp gaze onto him.

"My kid brother's grave says otherwise." I wasn't yelling, but I was close. "Tommy should be alive and well, but they didn't do his surgery because you wouldn't pay up."

Lis asked Ares something in Albanian, and he answered in kind. There was a hum from the other Albanians as father and son carried on a conversation, occasionally glancing my way. Then Lis turned to Ricky.

"You agreed to pay for the surgery?" he asked.

Ricky gulped under Lis's interrogation. "I—yeah. But that was for three cars. We only got two."

"Only because you and your lackeys weren't at the drop on time," I said. "I did my part, then had to wait around, and you left me there to get busted."

"No one told you to leave it on the fuckin' street for all that time so the cops could ID the plates," Ricky sneered. "Rookie move. You deserved to get pinched."

"For being loyal? For keeping my word? Nah, I didn't deserve shit," I retorted.

"You could have driven it around the block, you dumb fuck."

"And you could have showed the fuck up!" I shoved back from the table, about ready to pounce, room full of thugs or not.

Ricky was up a moment later, and more than one person in the room had their hands inside jackets or under shirts, reaching for their pieces if the worst happened.

Then Lis barked something else in Albanian, and silence fell. I couldn't have translated worth a damn, but in my experience, "shut the fuck up" sounded about the same in every language.

"You had an agreement," he reiterated to Ricky. "Michael did his part. You did not. This is the truth."

A quick glance from Ares made me wonder if he had a part in this particular judgment.

Ricky's face flushed an even brighter shade of red. "Yeah, but he didn't finish the job! The cops grabbed the last car—"

"Because it sat on the street for an extra four hours, you crooked piece of shit," I cut in. "If you'd been there on time, you would have gotten your car, I'd never have been locked up, and my little brother might still be alive."

Ricky glared like he wanted to shoot me between the eyes. I stood straighter, daring him to come for me. I would have been more than happy to shove my fist right through his face, maybe force him to get a few more gold teeth. Thinking about Tommy had that effect on me. Especially when I was staring at the asshole responsible for his death.

In the end, Ricky didn't have to make a move. Lis made it for him.

The boss barked something in Albanian over his shoulder. Immediately, the men on the couches stood.

Ricky's eyes bugged out in fear.

"No," he sputtered. "Lis, please. Come on, man, this happened a year ago."

"It was a *bese*," Lis said calmly. "A promise. And a man is nothing without his promise."

He repeated the order to his thugs, who yanked Ricky away from the table and shoved him toward the exit.

"Lis, please!" Ricky shouted. "I'll make it up to him, I swear it! I'm good, man—don't do thi—"

His cries were silenced when the door slammed shut behind him. Beside me, Paul and Jay looked like they wanted to melt into the floorboards.

I focused on Lis, who was sitting there as calm as ever, as if he hadn't just ordered a man to, well, I didn't know what, exactly. But I was pretty sure if I did, I'd be in even more shit.

He looked me over with a critical eye. "You don't let people push you around, Michael Scarrone."

I shrugged. What was I supposed to say to that?

"You keep your promises," he continued. "And you keep quiet."

He glanced to Ares, who seemed to nod in agreement, then to a few other men, who did the same. I didn't like the feeling that they were having an unspoken conversation. Even more that it seemed to be a decision about me.

"We could use someone like you," Lis said. "Someone with integrity. Someone we can trust. And with your job, your position—"

"No," I interrupted, though that dread was seeping into my chest, my heart, with a finality I truly hated. "I told Paul. I told Ricky. And now I'm telling you. The Zolas are straight. They don't deserve to be dragged into the life if they don't want it. I won't do that to them."

Another few glances were shared around the table. But not a word was spoken in Albanian or any other language.

Which meant that they had already come to a conclusion before I'd even stepped into the room.

Which meant Lis Antoni had already known what I'd say.

"Okay," he said. "You work for me, and I leave the cars alone. Good deal. Good for me, good for you, yes?"

The dread fell to my stomach like a stone and stayed there.

It was a sentence no different than the one the judge had handed down.

"I…" I shook my head, internally grasping for excuses. Anything to get me out of this. Out of this room. Out of this city. Out of this fuckin' life.

A pair of green eyes blinked at me, bright and beautiful.

Oh, God, Lea.

I'd miss her. I really would.

"Can I think it over?" I asked.

Lis shrugged, like he knew it wouldn't matter. "Two days."

It was the best I could do. There was no real way to say no to someone like this. All I could maybe get was time.

Which really meant figuring out how to say goodbye to Lea and the rest of the Zolas.

Just because I was condemned to either a life with

the mob or one on the lam didn't mean I had to drag her down with me.

I'd never do that to her.

I'd never do that to someone I was pretty sure I loved.

NINETEEN

AND NEVER STAND A WOMAN UP WHEN SHE MAKES YOU DINNER

Lea

Michael was late.

Not ten minutes or so.

The clock in Nonna's kitchen read nearly nine fifteen. The manicotti I'd made using her recipe and homemade sauce were getting cold. The salad was wilted. And I had been sitting miserably at the kitchen table in my favorite sage-colored mini dress and the gold heels I borrowed from Angie, feeling like an absolute idiot while I watched the minutes tick by.

Not for the first time since meeting the broody new mechanic in my grandfather's shop, I wished I had a cell phone. More than that, I wished Michael had a number. A pager. A landline. Anything I could call if only to cuss him out.

I wasn't the queen of England, but I was a Zola. No one stood me up. No one.

The minute hand moved past the five.

I gave up on pretending to study and stood, my chair screeching loudly across the linoleum floor.

"Fuck this," I announced to the room. "And fuck him."

I grabbed the manicotti from the table and brought it into the kitchen, where I proceeded to dump as much of it into the trash as I could.

That was when the doorbell rang.

"What?" I snapped before I marched down the hall and yanked open the front door. "I swear to God, Michael, if it isn't you on the other side—"

"It's me, Tess."

I opened the door fully to reveal Michael standing sheepishly on the porch, looking more like he'd just rolled out from under a car than gotten ready for a date. He was still wearing his coveralls, the top tied around his waist so he could throw his black jacket over the thin undershirt that didn't exactly hide much of his physique or tattoos. He looked rumpled but still gorgeous. I hated that I had to admit it to myself.

"I—I wasn't going to come," he admitted. "I shouldn't even be here, but—"

"What do you mean, you shouldn't be here?" I demanded.

"I mean, we can't see each other anymore, Lea. I wasn't even going to come over, but you deserve more than being stood up. So I'm here, and I'm sorry, but it can't work between us. You know it, and I know it, and that's how it's got to be."

He turned to leave but didn't get more than a step before I grabbed the back of his coveralls and pulled hard.

"Fuck!" he snapped, barely catching his balance on the slick front step. The temperature had dropped, and things out there were getting icy. "Goddammit, Lea, let go."

"Not until you tell me what the hell is going on," I demanded. "I thought we sorted all this out last night. We had plans. We had a date. So what happened that made you decide all over again that you can't see me anymore, huh?"

Michael opened his mouth as if to argue with me, but then his eyes seemed to take me in all the way. The time I'd taken to curl my hair over my shoulders. The dress and shoes I'd borrowed from Angie this morning. The lipstick on my mouth, the bronzer on my cheeks, and the tiny bit of scent I'd dabbed under my jaw.

Maybe it was in my head, but I really felt like he could see it all.

His eyes shone, but I didn't think it was the moonlight or the streetlamps that did it.

"You dressed up," he said.

I looked down at my dress, then back at him. "Well, yeah. Just like I made dinner, cleaned my house, and took a freaking shower, for crying out loud. Because this was supposed to be a date. And until an hour ago, I kind of thought you were my boyfriend. I'm not the type to give up once I got a man. You have to put in the effort when you care about someone, Michael. You have to—mmmph!"

Suddenly, his lips were on mine, and Michael Scarrone was kissing every angry statement out of my head, erasing the past two hours with the firm lips and dizzying tongue that had invaded my thoughts for the last twenty-four.

As much as I wanted to resist, I melted into his embrace. Lord, the boy could kiss. His strong arms enveloped me, and I twined my fingers through the tousled strands of his hair. Belmont dissolved into a pool of iridescent lights and muddled noises—all I could feel was this man, this touch, this kiss.

When we finally separated, breathless and flushed, Michael touched his forehead against mine. His stormy eyes bored into mine, filled with vulnerability and determination.

"I'm sorry," he whispered. "I'm sorry I was late. You—Jesus, look at you."

I looked down at our entangled bodies, then back up, my cheeks flushing. "It's a dress."

"That you wore for me. You did this all for me. And I repaid you by…" He shook his head. "Fuck. I'm so sorry."

I traced a finger down his crooked nose. "You tried to break up with me. Again, I might add. Why do you keep doing that?"

He heaved a long sigh. "I keep trying to tell you I'm not the best person for you to be involved with. And it is the truth, even if you keep talking me back out of believing it."

All I could do was roll my eyes.

"Well, stop doing that," I said right before he kissed me again. "It never works. You should have learned that by now."

I pulled him into the house, walking backward as the door swung shut behind us.

"I'm getting your dress dirty," he murmured against my neck.

"You'll have to save up and buy Angie another one. And next time, take a shower and get dressed like a gentleman," I replied, though my hands wrapped around his neck and held him equally close.

"Yes, ma'am." He stopped, looked toward the kitchen, and sniffed. "You cooked."

"Well, yeah. I said I'd make you dinner."

I expected more bickering, followed by more soul-searing kisses, but instead, Michael took my hand and strode to the back of the house. There, he looked over the table, still set with our dishes, the burned-out candles, and the salad and bread, and then to the empty casserole pan next to the sink.

"You made me a real dinner. Set the table and everything."

I nodded, still confused by his confusion. "Well, yeah. That was the general plan, wasn't it?"

"And you dressed up. Did your hair and makeup and all."

I swallowed and nodded again. "Um, yeah." What was the big deal? I was starting to feel self-conscious.

He shoved a hand through his hair and muttered something that sounded like "I'm such a fuckin' asshole" before going into the kitchen to see for himself what happened to the pasta.

"You—I—"

"Michael, what is it?" I followed him in, utterly confused.

Both hands were shoved into his hair now, brown

eyes shining. Then he reached out and pulled me to him again.

"Thank you," he said softly against my lips. "No one's ever done anything like that for me before."

"What about Gina?" I asked before considering that maybe I didn't want to know the answer to that question.

A frown flashed across his face. "Hell fuckin' no. Gina never does anything for anyone but herself." He shook his head, like he was shaking away some memory. "I don't want to think about Gina right now, babe. I don't want to think about anything but you. Right here."

A flash of pain—and maybe regret—crossed his face but disappeared as he looked over the kitchen.

"You made me dinner," he pointed out yet again.

I rolled my eyes. "Most of it's in the trash. I, um, dumped it out right before you knocked on the door."

That crooked smile I was starting to love so much appeared. "I deserved that. Is there anything left, or should I get a fork and eat it out of the trash?"

I grimaced. "You would eat pasta out of the garbage?"

The smile shifted into a full-on grin. "If you made it, I would. I would eat dog food if you made it for me, baby girl. I'd be thankful for scraps."

"Well, no need for that." I moved for the fridge. "The antipasti made it. And there is still salad on the table, and maybe fusilli left from last night—hey!"

I found myself spun around as the fridge shut behind me. Michael picked me up by the waist and set me on the counter, then settled himself between my legs. One hand snaked around the nape of my neck, bringing me close for a kiss.

Once again, I was left totally breathless.

"Thank you," he said again. "And I'm sorry I wasn't here to enjoy what you made. I'm an asshole."

He kissed me again.

"Yes, you are," I mumbled, though I was now hungry for more than kisses. "Don't do it again."

"Gonna have to make it up to you." His voice was rough and heavy before he nipped my lower lip.

"Without a doubt." He tasted like peppermints and ice.

"Everyone's gone?"

I didn't think he would stop what he was doing, even if they weren't.

My fingers slipped through his dark hair. "Yeah, everyone's gone. It's just us now."

A mischievous grin tugged at the corners of his lips. "Good."

In that second, the tortured man living above my grandpa's garage disappeared. For once, I saw the boy Michael could have been—full of mischief, joy, even a bit of glee.

It was intoxicating.

My heart raced as his hands moved to my thighs, pulling me closer to the edge of the counter. The anticipation and desire mingled in the air, creating a tantalizing tension between us.

"Tell me what you want," he whispered against my ear, his warm breath sending shivers down my spine.

I bit my lip, unable to form words as his hands traveled higher, teasingly close to where I craved him most.

My body trembled with a mix of longing and excitement.

His voice was low and husky as he continued to tease me. "Should I guess?"

I nodded, unable to speak.

His fingers danced along the inside of my thigh, igniting a fire within me that burned hotter with each passing second. His touch was electric, sending jolts of pleasure through every nerve ending in my body.

"Is it this?" he murmured, his fingers inching closer and closer to my center.

I moaned softly, my head falling back as he slowly stroked me through the fabric of my panties. My body arched into his touch, silently begging for more.

He chuckled seductively. "No? How about this?" His thumb brushed against my clit, applying just enough pressure to make me gasp.

"Yes," I whimpered, barely able to get the word out.

My body hummed. I shoved off his coat, then twined my fingers in the soft cotton of his undershirt. The fabric strained against the sculpted muscles of his chest and arms, making him look like a god among men. His tattoos snaked around both arms, swirling around broad shoulders, cut muscles, straining forearms, and disappearing down his chest.

He paused, and I held my breath, wondering if he was going to leave me again or reveal that this was all some cruel joke. But then he growled with pure desire as he slid my panties down my legs, over my heels, and down to the floor.

"I need to taste you," he said as he pushed me to lean back on the counter.

My skirt slipped up my thighs, followed by the brush of his lips.

"Michael?" My voice was halfway between a warble and a purr. Once again, we were in completely new territory.

"Trust me, Tess."

His lips brushed against my inner thighs before settling on my clit. My body trembled as those large hands roamed over every inch of me, mapping out my curves with an expert touch. I couldn't control the moans as he settled his mouth over the core of me, licked and sucked, sending waves of pleasure throughout my body.

"Yes," I begged, my hands gripping his dark hair as I urged him on. He added one finger, then another, until I was filled completely, calling his name as I reached the brink of ecstasy.

But he didn't stop there. He kept pushing me higher and higher, his voice a deep rumble against my most sensitive parts.

"Let go, my contessa," he commanded. "My queen. Let it all go."

And so I did. Writhing on his face, I exploded in a frenzy of pleasure that left me weak and quivering in his arms. Right there on my grandmother's counters, without a thread of shame about me.

Eventually, Michael drew me back to reality and then kissed his way back up my body until he was seated between my legs once again.

It only made me want more. "Come here..." I spread my thighs, pulling him closer.

One broad hand wove its fingers into my hair before

he kissed me. "What do you want, baby? What can I give you?"

I felt drunk on the taste of him. The taste of me on him.

"I want…you," I whispered before biting lightly on his bottom lip.

He groaned. "Christ, Lea. Here?"

"Upstairs." I set his hands on my thighs, urging him to take what he so obviously wanted if the strain of his pants was any indication.

Me, I wanted to sink into him, wanted to dive into his very soul until he knew the truth that I was only starting to figure out for myself.

That I was his. He was mine.

There was no running from this connection. There never had been.

Michael swallowed. "I—Lea…"

Suddenly, all I wanted was for him to let go the way he'd allowed me to. Michael Scarrone had never had a safe place to land his entire life. I wanted to be that for him more than I'd ever wanted anything.

"Say it," I said, reaching out to caress his face. "Whatever it is, I'll listen."

He swallowed, his hard, dark eyes dancing over my face.

"I love you," he whispered thickly. "Is that crazy? I mean, I know we just met. I know we've barely—but you've done things no one—I've told you things that no one—shit. I'm not very good at this."

The broad hand around my thighs gripped even harder. He was so tough, so impermeable on the outside. But the vulnerability etched over those strong features broke my heart.

I cupped his face and placed a soft kiss on his lips.

"It's not crazy," I told him. "It's not crazy because I love you too."

His eyes widened, and for a moment, his expression turned to shock. But then it softened into relief, and that bashful smile I adored so much pulled at the corner of his lips. "I knew it. I knew it the moment we met."

My fingers traced the edge of his jaw, feeling the roughness of his beard. "It's not crazy because we were always meant to be together. You said you felt like you were home with me. I feel the same way."

He swallowed hard, his eyes searching mine for the truth. "I want to be yours. I want to give you everything you deserve, Lea, everything you need. But I don't know if I can."

My hands gripped his shoulders, pulling him closer, feeling the warmth of his body against mine. The connection between us was undeniable, powerful, and everything I'd ever wanted.

"Right now, what I need is for you to take me upstairs," I murmured, my voice barely above a whisper, the words barely leaving my lips before being kissed away by his eager mouth. "Second floor, bedroom on the right. Mine's the bed in the corner."

His body quivered—with need or anticipation, I didn't know. But I was shivering too as he gathered me in his arms. Carefully, he carried me up the stairs of my childhood home and into my bedroom, where he laid me atop the faded comforter before stepping back to remove his boots and coveralls.

When I looked up at him, he was only in his boxers and undershirt, staring down at me with eyes filled with love and desire. He leaned down and kissed me gently at first, then tasting me as if he was trying to memorize my flavor. I wrapped my arms around his and pulled him closer, feeling his body pressed against me, his erection hard and urgent.

I felt his hand on my thigh, sliding up my dress slowly, teasingly, making me wet. I hissed when his fingers traced the inside of my legs before slipping my entire dress up and over my head.

"You too," I murmured, pulling at his clothes.

I watched, utterly rapt, as he yanked his undershirt over his head, revealing a tightly muscled torso completely covered with art. He took a deep breath, watching me, and then pulled down his black boxers, revealing the full length of his arousal. His need for me.

My breath was ragged as my thighs clenched together.

"Are you ready?" he asked, pulling a foil from his coveralls. Then he frowned. "What is it?"

I reached out, and he came to me immediately.

"What is it?" he wondered. "Baby, what's wrong?"

"I—I'm a virgin." I bit out the words. Maybe he would change his mind. Maybe he'd think I was only a kid.

But instead, he smiled and kissed my nose. "Pretty sure we've been over that a few times now."

I flushed. "I'm making sure you know what you're getting."

Michael's body quivered over me, shaking with contained mirth.

"Stop it!" I hissed, batting his shoulder. "It's not funny!"

"It's fuckin' hilarious," he practically hooted. "Oh shit, my girlfriend is the cutest fuckin' thing!"

I smacked him again, but this time, my heart wasn't into it. Because, of course, he'd said the thing. The word.

"So," I prodded. "I *am* your girlfriend?"

TWENTY

MICHAEL, YOU'RE NAKED

Lea

Michael burst out laughing, the rough, joyful sound echoing around my small bedroom, thrilling my heart even as I curled into myself.

Was he laughing at me?

Was it that ridiculous?

Then he kissed me again, and all doubts evaporated.

"Are you my girlfriend?" he demanded. "Are you my...Jesus. Lea. Girlfriend doesn't even cut it. I've known you for a few weeks, and you're already the love of my life."

That shut me up.

As quickly as it had emerged, the levity between us disappeared.

"How can you say that?" I wondered. "You barely know me."

"How can you say you love me too?" he wondered

right back as he sat back on his heels at the end of my bed to look me over.

Instinctively, I sat up too and grasped for my sheets to cover my naked body. They didn't do much.

"How can you invite me up here?" he continued. "Sit with me, naked as the days we were born, and offer me your…what no one else has ever had from you?"

I hated the fear that crept into those deep eyes with every question he asked. It had me tossing the sheets aside so that I could scramble closer to him, wrap my arms around his neck, and let him know he was worthy of everything I had to give him.

It wasn't much. It was only me.

But it was something.

"I said I love you because it's the truth," I said. "Maybe for some people, it grows gradually, like a plant. But for us, it was fire. Immediate sparks. And then we both blew on the flame, and it exploded." I bit back a smile. "I think I loved you the second I watched you wolf down Nonna's pasta. You were so grateful. You didn't hold back."

"Neither did you," he said with a half-smile. "I probably loved you the second I saw you in the break-room, walking around like you owned it. I wanted you to own me."

We gazed at each other for a long time, green eyes meeting brown, reflecting wonder and love back at each other.

And then sparking with something else.

I looked down his body. Took in the twisting designs decorating his arms and torso. Toyed with the chain hanging from his neck. And then looked down at the rest of him.

"Michael," I said. "You're naked."

His dark eyes gleamed. "We're both naked, contessa." His eyes dipped down my body and back up before he delivered a quick kiss. "And for what it's worth, you look fuckin' amazing without clothes on."

My body heated as he kissed me again, this time with his tongue that had me begging for more.

Visions of what he had done to me on my family's kitchen counter danced through my mind. My core throbbed in response.

"I can feel your—it—on my leg," I whispered as he drifted his lips over my jaw.

His mouth curved into a smile against my neck. "You can say it out loud, you know."

"I know that," I snarled, though it only made him chuckle. "I can say the word 'cock.' I'm a virgin, not a prude. There's a difference."

"Oh, God, babe. Don't I fuckin' know it." His shoulders shook all over again with repressed laughter.

Suddenly, I was laughing too. Even as he continued to press kisses over my shoulders, down my chest, lingering over the small peaks of my breasts.

"I didn't realize it could be like this, though," I remarked as I combed my fingers through his hair. It was so soft and silky, like a pelt.

"Like what, Tess?"

"Fun. Funny. I didn't think it—sex—was really something people laughed about."

Michael's full mouth curved lopsided as he considered the statement. "I think it only happens on special occasions," he said before kissing me again. "With very special people who love each other like fuckin' crazy."

I pulled him closer, then back down to the bed so he was on top of me again. I didn't feel like laughing anymore.

We lay like that, kissing while our bodies got accustomed to each other. Until my skin seemed to blend with his, and his heaviness on top of me felt normal and good.

His left hand traveled up and down the length of my side, exploring the dips and curves of my thighs, hips, waist. It covered my breast completely, squeezing lightly as he groaned into my mouth.

I gasped when his hips tilted toward me, and the solid length of him slipped between my legs, like a key looking for its lock.

"Oh!" I gasped. "You're—"

"I'm right here, baby," Michael agreed before leaning down to take my other nipple between his teeth. He sucked lightly, and the shock of mild pain made my hips rise off the mattress of their own accord and grind into him.

Want rioted through my body and right between my legs as the tip of him teased my entrance. The world outside my twin bed didn't exist anymore. Everything I could possibly need was right here.

"Are you—are you sure you want to do this?" Michael's voice shook slightly, and the muscles in his armed flexed as he hovered over me.

I gulped. "Y-yes. Please."

That delicious smirk reappeared. "I know you're serious when you say 'please.'"

"Do it," I snapped before I could help myself. Then I yanked him down for another kiss and pulled him closer. "I need it."

That seemed to be his undoing.

He reached to the ground for the foil packet he had dropped there earlier. The sight of one had sent me running the one time Victor had brought it out. This time, however, I wasn't going anywhere.

I watched, half-curious, half-eager, as Michael rolled it over himself. He was beautiful, lean muscles straining with want, his tattooed skin gleaming in the light shining through the window. But it was really the expression in his eyes that had me transfixed, the complex blend of awe, desire, and, yes, love. That anyone would ever look at me like that seemed like a miracle. Even more so when I realized I was watching him the exact same way.

"Come here," I said softly when he was finished.

And then he was there, poised at my entrance, as his lips found mine again. So slowly I could hardly feel him move, he eased his way in, searching my face constantly for any signs of discomfort.

"You okay?"

"Michael?"

He stopped moving. "Yeah?"

I grabbed his hips. "Just do it."

Another second passed. And then he leaned down, kissed me with everything he had, and pushed all the way in.

I won't lie. It hurt. A lance of pain that would have stolen my breath if it hadn't already been taken by Michael's soft lips. He held perfectly still, his own muscles quivering, while he waited for me to breathe properly again.

"Okay?" His breath was sweet against my face.

I nodded. "I—yeah."

His face twisted with regret. "I can stop—"

"No," I interrupted quickly. "Oh—ah! Um, give me a minute. And maybe kiss me again."

That sweet smile crept back in. "I can do that."

It was as if he knew there was something about his kiss that wiped all my worries from my mind. It relieved the tension inside me.

The pain began to fade, replaced by a sensation of fullness and pressure. It wasn't pleasant, but it wasn't unbearable. Michael's eyes locked with mine as he held himself still. There was a mix of emotions there—love, desire, and a quiet determination. He was focused entirely on me, making sure I was okay.

I reached up and gently ran my fingers through his hair, pulling him down to kiss me again. I needed him to help me forget the pain for a moment. His kiss could help me forget anything.

And then, slowly, he began to move. His hips swayed as he found a rhythm, his thrusts deep and slow. I could feel each movement, the friction of our bodies joining together, heightening the intensity of the sensations.

The pain was still there, a constant reminder of the boundary we had crossed. But it receded a bit with every thrust. My hips met his, and I could feel myself becoming more aroused as our bodies moved together, lost to the world around us.

The room faded away. It was Michael and me,

locked in this moment, experiencing something raw and unfiltered.

Waves of pleasure began to build. Heat starting to spread throughout my entire body. Michael's eyes locked onto mine, and I could see the same hunger and desire reflected back at me.

"Michael," I whispered. I grabbed his hips, urging him to go faster, harder, deeper.

Michael's eyes never left mine as he continued to move, his breath ragged and his expression full. I whispered his name. And then proceeded to lose myself completely.

"Michael!" I shouted as that wave broke once more. I clawed for purchase, and he groaned along with me as we broke together again and again.

Michael groaned and buried himself into me one last time. He held us there, locked together, as my body shuddered around him.

Eventually, our breathing began to regulate, and the intensity of the moment began to fade. Michael's eyes never left mine; his expression filled with a mix of love, tenderness, and awe.

"I love you," he whispered. "Christ, Lea. I love you so fucking much. Do you understand?"

A tear slipped down my cheek as I nodded. I couldn't have explained why I was crying, but I realized I didn't have to as he gently kissed it away.

"Are you okay?" His voice was muffled against my skin.

"Yes. Better than okay. You?"

"Baby, I don't think I have ever been better in my

whole life." He pressed one final kiss to my lips. "I honestly don't think I could love anyone more."

My chest warmed.

He pulled out, and I felt a strange mix of satisfaction and sorrow as I watched him get up. The pain was gone, replaced with the ever-growing realization that I had crossed a line that could never be uncrossed.

He disposed of the condom into the little bin next to my desk, then returned to the bed and gathered me into his chest, allowing me to listen to his heart regulate while both our breathing slowed, long and relaxed.

This wasn't what anyone in my family would have wanted for me. I was supposed to do better. Follow in my brother's footsteps to college. They would say I was lowering myself, falling for a mechanic with a record, someone who would undoubtedly hold me back.

But I couldn't find it in me to be sorry.

And the future I saw with this man could never be limiting. Not if he loved me like this.

"I don't want to move," I admitted, my voice barely above a whisper.

Michael chuckled. "Neither do I."

We would have to, eventually. The rush of the streets outside were pressing against my window pane. Eventually, my family would come back, the world outside this bedroom would return, and we would have to figure out how to deal with it all.

But that could wait another few minutes.

Michael's arm tightened around my shoulders, urging me to relax into his big, strong body.

"I got you, Tess," he whispered into my hair. "Always. You can relax."

And so I gave myself up to the bliss and shut out the future for another moment or two. Or forever. That sounded nice.

And it was. It was perfection.

Until a few hours later, when we were awakened by a very loud voice.

"What," roared my grandfather, who *never* yelled, "the hell are you doing with my granddaughter?"

TWENTY-ONE

THE DESALINIZATION PROJECT; OR, WORST CASE SCENARIO

Michael

At the sound of Mattias Zola's booming voice, I was out of Lea's bed faster than a bullet from a shotgun.

Wrong move.

I mean, fuckin' historically wrong move.

Because that had me standing naked in Lea Zola's bedroom. Naked in front of her grandpa. Naked in front of her grandma. Naked in front of all four of her sisters.

"Mamma mia," muttered Mrs. Zola as she tried in vain to put her hands over the eyes of the little ones, who immediately squirmed out of arm's reach.

"Oh my God! Lea's in here with a guy!" shouted the one whose name was Frankie.

Joni, Marie, Frankie, and Kate.

Good thing I remembered their names since they were all fucking staring at me.

"You can see his thingy!" cried the youngest, whose name I remembered was Joni.

"Ew!" yelled Marie, as she pointed at my dick. "It's right there!"

I grabbed something—anything—to cover up. It happened to be a blue folder labeled "Desalinization Project."

"Yo, could you not play 'hide the sausage' with my lab report?" Kate drawled. "I'd prefer not having to lie to my biology teacher about the dried jizz."

"Katie!" scolded her grandmother. "Don't say 'jizz' in front of your sisters!"

"What's 'jizz'?" asked Joni. "Is it like when a boy says he's gonna 'take a whizz'?" She pointed a little finger at me. "Did you pee in my sisters' room?"

"Ew!" Marie yelled again. "He peed in Lea's bed! Why did you do that?"

"GET OUT!" Lea shrieked from the bed, her bedsheet wrapped around her body.

God, she was beautiful in the morning.

Because it was, in fact, morning. Eight a.m., according to the clock on her bedside table. Which meant that after I'd declared my undying love for this girl and taken her virginity instead of breaking up with her the way I'd intended, we hadn't just stolen a few extra minutes together but had slept like babies for the rest of the damn night. And woken up, like idiots, to this shit show.

Jesus. I was a fuckin' idiot.

Best night of sleep I ever had, though.

Before I could do anything, though, Mattias Zola strode into the room, grabbed me by the throat, and shoved me against the wall beside the tiny closet that Lea shared with her sister. Solid move. Dude was quick for an old guy.

"You," he growled. "You…here…with my grand-daughter! You lousy…no-good…*'nzevato*!" His speech disintegrated into a torrent of what I recognized as the Neapolitan dialect my grandmother had sometimes spoken before she died. "*Sicchio e lota! Vafammocc a mammata!*"

I didn't know what any of it meant, but by the way his wife's face turned an ungodly shade of red, I knew it was nothing good.

I straightened with as much dignity as I could muster while standing bare-ass naked with a lab report guarding my dick like a fig leaf on a statue in the Vatican.

"Mr. Zola," I said. "Mattias—"

"Don't think you can come in here and disrespect my family and say my name," he gritted through his teeth, shoving his beefy forearm into my throat.

It took everything I had not to fight back. Had it been anyone else—literally anyone else—they would have been on the floor, and I'd serve up a taste of their own medicine.

Instead, I was having my naked ass handed to me by a geezer probably forty years my senior and sucking it the fuck up.

For her, of course. It was always for her.

"Okay, man." I held up one hand—using both would have bared everything I had to the family. "Okay. You got it. But I don't mean any disrespect, Mr. Zola. Honest, I don't."

"He has a lot of tattoos," one of the girls remarked from the doorway. I couldn't see who over Mattias's hat, but I thought it was Frankie.

"I like them," Joni said with a dreamy sigh. "'Specially all over his muscles."

"Ew," Marie said for the third time. "You're so gross."

"Get out!" Lea shouted for the second time, and this time, she crossed the room to yank her grandfather off me. "Nonno, let him go!"

"And leave you alone with him? No, no, no," Mattias snapped, his eyes boring into me like fiery drills.

Lea snorted. "What are you worried about? Obviously, the worst has already happened, Nonno. My innocence is gone. Your good girl is ruined, okay?"

I shot her a "What the hell, Lea?" look. On the other side of the room, Kate snorted. But honestly, I didn't need her to remind the guy that I'd been in bed with his granddaughter two seconds earlier.

My girl had some brass balls, that was for sure. Clearly, it was a family trait.

"Let us get dressed, all right?" she said, still clutching the purple sheets to her chest. "Then we'll come down, and you can give us all the hell you want."

I had to give it to her. My girl slipped right into boss mode, naked or not, and I'd never been so damn glad for it. Everyone in the family seemed to respond to her simple commands like they always did—even the man in charge.

Mattias didn't move his gaze from mine, but his jaw tightened even more as I watched him consider Lea's words.

"Mattias," called Mrs. Zola before she said something softly in Italian.

Mattias's steely anger loosened a few degrees.

"You got two minutes," he told me. "And I'm gonna be standing right. Out. Side."

He jammed his arm into my throat once more for good measure before dropping it, leaving me wheezing against the wall while he muttered more Neapolitan obscenities on his way out.

"Lea," Mrs. Zola said sharply.

We both faced her as the smaller girls followed their grandfather out of the room. I expected another dressing down, this one from Lea's nonna. But instead, Mrs. Zola silently jerked her head toward the window, then switched her sharp gaze onto me.

Her meaning was clear. My best bet wasn't to take whatever Mattias Zola had for me like a man but to scurry out the window like a scared rat.

Lea held her sheet even tighter to her chest. She didn't argue, though.

"Kate, come with me," said Mrs. Zola sharply.

"But it's my room!" Kate complained, clearly annoyed that she had to leave the scene of the crime too. But she obeyed anyway, calling over her shoulder as she went, "I'd like a new folder for that lab report while you're out, please, *Michael!*"

And then the door closed, and miraculously, Lea and I were left alone.

Lea located some pajama pants and a T-shirt from a bureau beside her bed while I sprang for my coveralls, cursing myself that I hadn't even changed before coming here last night. Now, I was expected to climb out the window like a criminal? I couldn't have come up with a worse way to ingratiate myself to the family. Maybe I could leave a note.

Which would say what?

Hey, Mattias, how you doing? That's right, I'm still an ex-con with about twenty dollars to my name and nowhere to live but your upstairs breakroom. By the way, I'm giving it to your grand-daughter now. Yeah, the one you explicitly told me to stay away from. Also, I'm nothing but a grease monkey who can't even put on a clean pair of pants to enter your home.

Fuck.

"You'd better go," Lea said behind me. "I've seen him like this before, once, when he caught Mattie sneaking his girlfriend out after curfew. And he doesn't even like Sherry."

"It's not like he doesn't know exactly where to find me," I grumbled as I yanked on my boots.

Lea shrugged as she shrugged into her robe. "It's better to give him a few days."

When I was finished tying my boots, I stood up to find her opening the window. She had every intention of following her grandmother's suggestion.

Out the window. Down the drainpipe.

No more than I was worth.

"Lea!" stormed Mattias from downstairs. "It's been two minutes!"

"You'd better go," she said again, then popped up onto her toes and pressed a kiss to my cheek. "I'll come to the garage when he's done."

"If he doesn't kick me out first," I mumbled as I headed toward the window.

Briefly, I contemplated where the hell else I would

go if not the garage. Back to the church, I supposed. Father Deflorio might have a place for me. Otherwise, it would have to be a friend's couch if I could still find one. Worst-case scenario, a shelter.

"Hey."

I turned around after opening the window and found Lea watching me.

She touched a hand to my knuckle. "I love you."

I wondered, if I asked her, would she follow me?

I didn't have time to find out.

"Lea!"

The doorknob turned.

"Go," she ordered.

And I flew.

I hadn't gone two blocks when the snow started to fall.

TWENTY-TWO

FOOTSTEPS IN THE SNOW

Lea

There were still only flurries outside when I heard Nonno announce he was going to close up the garage for the day and get it ready for a potential snow-storm. The last time a blizzard hit the city, a pipe burst and flooded his whole office. That was four years ago.

"Please check on Michael!"

The first words I'd spoken all night flew out of my mouth while I hammered down the stairs. Nonno stopped in the front doorway, allowing a few errant flakes inside while Kate looked up from her book on the couch.

Nonno closed the door and faced me.

I knew what he was going to say. That it was rich of me to start speaking now when I wanted something. Not two hours ago, when he and Nonna had lectured me until my ears were bleeding on the sin of premarital sex, the dangers of a criminal like Michael, and all the things that might happen to me, from an unplanned pregnancy to going straight to hell, all because of a boy.

I hadn't spoken. I hadn't had anything to say. At least not anything that they wanted to hear. They didn't care that I was in love. They didn't know Michael like I did.

And I wasn't sorry. Not even a little bit.

Now, though, I had to use my voice.

"He's—I know you're mad, Nonno. But it's cold. The city just issued a blizzard warning, and he doesn't have anywhere else to go. It's the right thing to do, and I…I want to make sure he's safe."

Out of the corner of my eye, I caught Kate cringing.

"Lea, do you even know if he went back to the garage?" she wondered. "Would he actually go there after what happened?"

I honestly didn't know. He had probably stopped in, if only to get what few things he had, but other than that, I didn't know where else he would go, either. Someone who was living in his boss's garage didn't have a lot of options.

"Stop."

We all turned. Nonno's face was bright red under his old-fashioned fedora, though his voice hadn't lifted a decibel. A good sign. At least he wasn't yelling anymore.

My grandfather's eyes softened as he looked at me, and for a moment, I saw a flicker of understanding. He sighed heavily and nodded.

"Okay," he finally said, his tone begrudging. "I'll

check for him. But this changes nothing, Lea. Not a one."

I launched down the stairs and wrapped Nonno in a hug. "Thank you," I whispered fiercely into his ear.

He stiffened but eventually returned the squeeze.

It was the first sign I got that things would be all right again.

"And don't—please don't hurt him?" I couldn't help but add.

Nonno extracted himself enough to deliver a particularly scathing look. One that clearly said I had no place to warn him about anything.

I had the decency to blush. He called his goodbye in Italian to Nonna before shutting the door behind him.

FOUR HOURS LATER, Nonno hadn't come back.

I had called the garage six times and only received the same voicemail with Nonno's gruff message on it again and again. I even yelled as loud as I could on the voicemail, hoping the sound would carry up to the breakroom, where Michael might hear me.

Either he wasn't there, or things were too intense to answer.

I wasn't sure which was worse.

"That's it," I said, grabbing my coat. "I'm going over there."

"Lea, no," Nonna chided from the couch, where she was darning a pair of Nonno's socks. "That's a bad idea."

"It's a fine idea," I said. "I can't sit here and wonder

if something went wrong between them. I need to know."

My grandmother huffed, then set her mending aside. "Okay, then I will come too." She stood and called up the stairs. "Kate! Lea and I are going to the shop to find your nonno! Watch the girls, okay?"

There was a shout of assent from the floor above.

I frowned. "Nonna, *that's* a bad idea. I can handle this mess myself. I'm the one who made it."

"And who will make sure your nonno listens, eh?" she demanded, as she threw on her own camel-colored wool coat. She shook her head. "I'm not saying what you do is right. And I'm not saying that this boy is a good idea. But I don't want you to run away either. If you're going, I will come with you."

I noticed that the one reason she didn't give was being worried about her husband. She didn't have to say it out loud. I felt the same way.

The frigid air bit at my cheeks as we trudged through the snow-covered streets toward the garage. Flurries still fell gently from the brightening sky, painting everything in a soft white blanket. It was eerily quiet, the only sound being the crunching of my boots against the icy pavement.

As we approached the familiar red door of Nonno's garage, my heart was already pounding. There was a clear set of footprints leading to and from the front door, but only one. I prayed that Michael's tracks had already been covered with snow, and he was still huddled inside where it was plenty warm.

Nonna handed me the key, and with shaky hands, I unlocked the door and opened it. The door creaked, revealing a dimly lit but empty garage complete with cars in progress, shelves stacked with tools and parts, and other equipment shoved against the walls.

It was almost as cold inside as outside, and I shivered involuntarily as I stepped inside.

"Michael?" I called.

No response.

"Mattias!" Nonna shouted.

The two cars being worked on remained silent.

The clip of Nonna's boots on concrete echoed through the garage as she strode into the office and flipped on a light. No one was there, of course. I skittered up the stairs to Michael's room, hoping the light was off because he was still asleep, not because no one was there.

No dice.

But he'd clearly been here. The room was empty and cold, but the bed was neatly made in the corner, and the few belongings he had were cleared out completely. Considering there were no tracks leading to or from the garage, that meant he had come and gone right after leaving the house this morning.

I returned downstairs to find Nonna waiting by the door.

"Where do you think they went?" I asked.

She shrugged. "I think the church. Father Deflorio sent Michael here in the beginning. Your nonno would go there to find him if he wasn't here." She pulled her gloves back on. "We will go home and wait."

"But—" I started.

"Home," she repeated in that tone that brooked no argument.

I reluctantly followed Nonna out of the garage, my mind spinning with worry and unanswered questions. But we'd barely started walking the longest two blocks ever back to the house before a voice called out from across the street.

"How you doin', mami?"

I turned to find a familiar-looking man making his way through the snow, with two men trailing him.

I knew him. Or at least, I knew his sister, Gina.

"Paul?" I asked as he approached us. "Reyes, right?"

Nonna tugged on my sleeve, but I shook her away. Reyes's companions circled outward to stand on either side of us, effectively caging us against the shop's entrance.

Shit.

"That's right," Paul congratulated me. "Been a while since I was in high school, yeah?"

Swallowing hard, I nodded. "I was probably a freshman."

Which meant there was no real way he would have known me back then.

"You wouldn't happen to know where your boyfriend went, would you, pretty?"

I frowned as a prickle of goose bumps flew up my back. "I don't know who you're talking about. I don't have a boyfriend."

Nonna's silent stare told me I had answered exactly right, but not because of her concerns about Michael.

Unfortunately, Reyes wasn't buying it.

"Hear that? She don't have a boyfriend," Reyes told his cronies, then looked back to me with an expression wholly different than his genial words. "Guess we'll have to test that out."

I backed up instinctively. "What does that mean?"

He grabbed my arm. "It means you're coming with me. Grandma too. No better way to catch a rat than with a big juicy trap."

TWENTY-THREE

YOU'D THINK THE MOB COULD AFFORD BETTER COUCHES

Lea

You learn to pick your battles when you live in Belmont. When I was fourteen, some guy tried to take my purse while I was waiting for the bus. It was a Coach bag I'd saved up for six months to buy on layaway from a consignment shop near Fordham. I wasn't letting that thing go without a fight—not at ten a.m. on a Saturday to a wannabe thug with nothing more than his hands and some good sneakers. Not when I was at a crowded stop with three of my friends to back me up. And not when I had a big brother who taught me exactly how to use a kick to the back of the knee to bring someone down.

But Paul Reyes and his friends weren't a bus-stop mugger, a deserted street after a blizzard wasn't a crowded street on a busy Saturday morning, and my little old grandma wasn't a bunch of teenagers and another ten strangers backing me up. So, this was not the battle I was willing to pick.

Which was how Nonna and I allowed ourselves to be hustled down the block to a freshly plowed 187th, where we were ushered into a battered SUV and quickly blindfolded as the car took off into the frozen city. Nonna's shaky hand grabbed for mine, and she kept it tightly in her grasp until we reached its destination. We were lugged out of the car and into a nondescript building before our blindfolds were finally removed.

Once we could see again, Nonna and I squinted, trying to adjust our eyes to the light. We were in a room containing a few threadbare couches surrounding a television. A man with slicked black hair and a yellow-checked hoodie was sitting at a battered wooden table, counting a stack of cash.

He looked up when we entered. "Paul, finally. Took you fuckin' long enough."

"She wasn't where she was supposed to be. Had to go on a goose chase." None too gently, Paul guided Nonna and me to one of the couches. "Sit."

We obeyed, though the sharp smell of mildew clinging to the couch made it difficult to breathe. Nonna trembled beside me, her frail hand tightening its hold on mine.

"What—what do you want from us?" I asked Paul, then looked at the man sitting at the table.

"Did you tell Carrera?" the man asked Paul, ignoring my question.

Paul nodded. "I paged Gina. She's putting the word out with everyone in the neighborhood. He'll find out."

"Who?" I asked. "What is it you want? I can't give you anything."

Finally, the man at the table turned to me with a glint in his eye and offered a smile that revealed two gold teeth. "It ain't you we want, sweetheart. I'm sorry you had to get mixed up in all this, but we're trying to catch a rat, see. And you are the sweetest piece of cheese he ever sniffed."

"Michael," Nonna whispered.

A new and very different type of fear bolted through my stomach.

Obviously, I knew that Michael hadn't walked a straight and narrow path. But I hadn't known he was still involved in criminal activities. And I had no doubt these men were absolutely criminal.

Nonna's trembling hand tightened around mine even more, seeking comfort and reassurance in our shared fear. The room seemed to close in on us, suffocating us with its heavy silence.

"What do you mean? What has Michael done?" I stammered, my voice barely above a whisper.

The man leaned back in his chair, a sinister smile playing on his lips. "Your sweetheart owes me a favor. More than one since he made a fool out of me. He thought he could run and hide, but little did he know we'd find the perfect bait to lure him back out again." His eyes scanned me with an unsettling intensity.

As dread consumed me, anger ignited within. What exactly had Michael done to earn this man's vengeance? What was the "favor" he was expected to pay back? But I knew that dwelling on these questions would get me nowhere. I had to focus on keeping Nonna safe and finding a way to help Michael.

"Please," I said, desperation coloring my voice. "Let my grandmother go. She has nothing to do with this. I'll do whatever you want. Just release her."

"Lea, no!" Nonna hissed.

"And have her running to the cops? Ricky, they must think you're real dumb," Paul chided, causing the other two men with him to chuckle too.

The man at the table—apparently known as Ricky —didn't seem to find it funny.

"She won't tell anyone," I tried again, completely lying through my teeth. "She barely speaks English anyway, and since we were blindfolded, she has no idea where we are, so—"

"Shut up!" shouted Ricky, slamming his hand on the table with a hard slap that echoed through the room. "Christ, do you ever fuckin' shut up?"

This time I actually did.

For a second, anyway.

"I don't think you need to—"

"Paul, gag this bitch," Ricky interrupted. "I don't want to hear her no more."

Seconds later, a musty cloth was looped around my mouth and secured behind my head while the gorillas with Ricky tied my hands together. They did the same thing with Nonna and then stood back to admire their work.

"Finally," Ricky said as he sat back down at the table. "I couldn't hear myself think over her yammering. I need a little peace and fuckin' quiet."

It didn't last long.

"Where is she, goddammit? Where the fuck is she?"

The voice was muffled but loud behind the thick door into the apartment. I screamed around the gag. Nonna's eyes blinked wide with recognition. I tried to yell his name again, though it was almost completely silenced around my gag.

Seconds later, the door shook upon impact several times. Then it splintered around the lock as it burst open, and Michael hurtled into the room.

"Lea!" he roared.

With a fierce battle cry, he lunged forward, his fist connecting with Paul's jaw with a satisfying crack. The other two men rushed at him, but he was quick and agile, dodging their attacks and countering with powerful blows. His movements were swift and calculated, as if he had been trained for this very moment. The room erupted into chaos, punches and grunts filling the air.

"Michael! Behind you!" I screamed into the gag, my voice barely intelligible.

One of the men managed to land a punch to Michael's side, causing him to stumble. But he quickly regained his footing, retaliating with a vicious uppercut that sent his attacker crashing to the ground.

The room fell into a brief silence. Ricky seemed frozen as he watched the scene unfold as knowing fear replaced the man's snotty arrogance.

It was then I noticed exactly where his line of sight led: to a gun lying innocuously on a shelf on the other side of the room.

I wriggled my bound hands, desperately trying to loosen the tight knots. Nonna caught on to my efforts and began squirming beside me, her hands trembling as she worked against her restraints.

Michael fought even harder, his punches becoming more precise and forceful. Blow after blow, he unleashed his fury upon the remaining man until there was nothing left but a crumpled heap of bodies on the floor.

Breathing heavily, Michael turned to us. "Lea, baby. Mrs. Zola," he said urgently, as he rushed over to untie us. "Are you okay? Did they hurt you?"

"We're fine," I managed once my gag was removed. "But Michael—the gun!"

He followed my gaze across the room. Then both he and Ricky made a mad dash for the weapon, knocking over chairs, tripping over bodies, and generally causing havoc wherever they went.

"Who?" demanded Nonna. "Who got it?"

"That would be me, *signora.*"

Ricky's voice slid down my back like a finger of ice.

"No," I whispered as I found him pointing the gun directly at Michael.

"You think you can fuck me over like that?" Ricky barked. "Throw me under the bus right in front of my boss? Do you even know how fuckin' hard it was not to end up in the fuckin' river, you piece of shit?"

"I told the truth," Michael said more calmly than I would have expected. His hands were up, almost like he was trying to tame a wild cat. "You were late. But *I'm* the one who did time because of it, remember?"

"And what do you think happened because of that, huh?" Ricky demanded, shaking the gun like a laser pointer. "The cops ain't that stupid, man. They traced the cars right back to the shop we had going, shut the whole thing down. I had to lay low for a year, and since then, nobody wants to touch me. No one." He pointed at Nonna and me. "They could help. Zola's got the space and wouldn't nobody suspect him of nothin'. You could help. You *should* help. But you won't, you selfish fuck."

"That's what this is about?" Michael looked legitimately shocked. "Your little chop shop got shut down, so you need a new one to cover your ass? The fuck, Ricky? It isn't my job to set you up."

"I got a quota to make!" Ricky shrieked. "You don't understand. You been gone for two years. These Albanians, man, they are crazy. They don't take no for an answer. They don't let *anyone* out! Including you, in case you forgot the last two days."

"What?" I croaked, glancing between Michael and Ricky. "Michael, what is he talking about?"

Michael looked at me, then back to Ricky. "He— he's right, Tess. I'm sorry."

My mouth dropped. So much made sense. That was why he appeared on my doorstep looking about as happy as Charlie Brown, trying to break up with me again. It hadn't only been about my grandfather's rules. He was trying to protect me, protect *us*. Always.

"Look, Rick, I'll help you," Michael was saying as he edged across the room, planting his body directly between Ricky and where Nonna and I were still cowered by the couches, now clutching each other's hands. "We'll get you up and going. But you got to let them go. Let Lea and her grandmother out of here, and you and me, we'll figure out the rest. I promise."

"Michael, *no*—"

"Hush, Tess." He delivered the order without even looking at me.

Nonna's hand around my wrist told me to do as he said.

For a moment, I thought the other man might agree.

The gun wavered, even dropping, as Ricky appeared to consider Michael's offer. I exhaled—maybe we would actually get out of here alive. Maybe it would all work out in the end.

But then Ricky looked up like a man possessed. "I said, don't *fuck* with me, Scarrone."

And then he pointed the gun directly at Michael.

"No!" I screamed, and before I could even stop to think, I launched myself over the back of the couch and on top of Michael, forcing him to the ground as the gunshot blasted through the apartment, followed by another crash.

I covered my beloved with my body, bracing myself for impact as I kept my head down.

But the bullet never came.

Only the sound of a very deep, Eastern European voice.

"I apologize for being late. It appears I've interrupted something."

I looked up, distracted enough that Michael was able to gently disentangle himself from me. Our eyes met, full of all the things we couldn't say in front of our audience.

"Stay here," he whispered, then stood to face the new intruders.

I got up and brushed myself off out of habit, only to be joined by Nonna, who grabbed my hand in a way that told me this time she would not be letting go.

"Lis," Michael greeted the middle-aged speaker. "Glad you could make it."

Lis—whoever he was—was accompanied by four large men dressed in varying outfits of black and gray, all holding firearms that were pointed at Ricky. Behind them was a younger man slouched in the doorframe who shared the same silver eyes as Lis—eyes that were currently fixed directly on me.

I blinked as our stares collided.

He quickly looked away.

"You called Lis?" Ricky's eyes bugged out of his head.

Michael smirked. "What, you didn't want your boss finding out about this little abduction, Ricky?" He shook his head. "Not so sly, asshole."

"Drop it." The man called Lis nodded at the gun still hanging limply from Ricky's hand.

The other four gorilla-shaped gentlemen held their guns steady. With a defeated sigh, Ricky set his gun on the ground.

Lis strode forward, his face a mask of cold fury as he kicked the gun back for his associates to pick up.

"You thought you could pull a stunt like this without me finding out?" Lis spat, his heavily accented voice laced with venom. "You're a fool. And dishonest too."

Ricky cowered under Lis's withering gaze. Beads of sweat formed on his forehead as he stammered, "I-I didn't mean any harm—I just wanted to teach Scarrone a lesson. He can't renege on a deal like that. It embarrassed Mancuso. The firm. The whole organization."

"No, it embarrassed you," Lis corrected him. He took a step closer, his eyes burning holes into the trembling man. "And you made a liar out of me. I never break my word, Riccardo. This is unacceptable."

Quick as a striking viper, Lis delivered an open-hand slap to Ricky's face that sent him sprawling to the floor.

"I know, I was wrong," Ricky whimpered, trying to shield himself as the others in the room watched. "I shouldn't have done it. I'm sorry."

Nonna's gaze darted around the room. Michael, however, stood tall as he faced Lis with unwavering determination.

"It's done now," he said, his voice steady and unyielding. "Ricky's mistakes have consequences. You can't deny that."

Lis's face was still hard and unreadable. "So they do."

He turned to the men who had accompanied him and barked at them in a language I didn't recognize, but sounded a lot like the Albanians in Belmont. Two sprang forward and grabbed Ricky, who immediately started squealing like a stuck pig as they dragged him from the apartment.

"Where are they taking him?" I couldn't help but wonder.

Nonna's hand immediately fell on my knee, and she shook her head. Michael also grabbed for my hand and squeezed a silent request for silence. Clearly, they were both on the same page—the one where it was better not to ask those kinds of questions.

"Nowhere good," Michael confirmed. "I wouldn't worry about him anymore."

After Ricky had been hauled away, Lis delivered another set of directions to his men. They moved toward the bodies strewn across the floor and started lugging them up and onto the other couch.

Then Lis turned to us and gave a meaningful look toward the door.

We didn't need any other direction. Michael carefully escorted Nonna up from the couch, then put an arm around me so he could guide us both from the room. He didn't seem to care that a cut over his eye was still bleeding or that the pocket in his coat was torn. We were obviously his only concern.

"Scarrone," Lis called.

Michael paused in the doorway and looked over his shoulder.

"An honest man deserves his freedom," Lis said in a voice that wasn't altogether unfriendly but still sent chills up my spine anyway. "For now. But one day, I will want a favor."

Michael seemed to think about that for a moment while the hand on my arm tightened ever so slightly. "One day," he said finally. "But that day is not today."

It seemed to be good enough for the mobster.

"No," Lis agreed. "A favor's no good until a man gives it on his own. Take your women home, Scarrone. You keep your promises. I can wait until you're ready to keep this one too."

TWENTY-FOUR

WELCOME HOME, MICHAEL

Michael

I t was strange, the way Lea's house was starting to feel so familiar but off-limits at the same time. The little brown house wedged between a brick apartment building and a trio of townhomes reminded me of the gingerbread houses they'd let us make in one of the group homes at Christmas. Nothing special. Expired graham crackers, cheap frosting, and dollar store candy. We weren't allowed to touch them for days after we made them, but it was the highlight of the year, one of the few times I could remember being happy as a kid.

After getting out of the cab that took us back to Belmont, we trailed behind Mrs. Zola, Lea's gloved hand firmly in mine while I reached out with the other, guarding in case the older woman slipped in the snow and ice. When we reached the front porch, I released Lea's hand.

"Now that you're home safe, I'll…" I trailed off, unsure of what to say.

What *would* I be doing? I was free in every sense of the word. But what was I supposed to do with that freedom?

In the last twenty-four hours, my life had changed too many times to count. And even though the shackles of the Mancuso-Antoni Organization were no longer threatening to hold me back, I doubted I was welcome in the house I wanted more than anything to enter.

"Where do you think you're going?"

Lea and I both turned at the sound of her grand-mother's voice. Sofia Zola was already heading up the front stoop.

As I looked up at the Zolas' warm home with its sagging eaves and crooked steps, I thought my heart was about to jump out of my chest; it was thumping so hard. This was worse than waiting for Lis to make his judgment. Worse than sitting before the parole board or in front of the judge. This felt like my real judgment day.

And all for the girl standing next to me.

"It'll be all right," Lea murmured, giving my hand a squeeze as Mrs. Zola unlocked the door.

"Will it?" I couldn't help but wonder.

I got no answer because as soon as the door opened, we stepped into a house full of chaos.

The living room was overrun with Zolas. Lea's smaller sisters were chattering around the sofa, watching some kind of show, while Kate seemed to be in some kind of argument with her grandfather as he and Matthew were in the middle of putting on coats to leave the house.

"I should go with you," Kate was saying. "Frankie can take care of the littles. You don't know where she hangs out. I can find Linda and Angie, and the three of us can hit up all of those spots."

"They won't be at the park or the Mall in a freaking blizzard, Kate. And where would that leave Nonna?" Matthew replied as he bent down to tie his Jordans. "Stay here."

"You never know," Kate argued back. "Nonna could be there with her."

Mrs. Zola cleared her throat. "Nonna is right here. Lea too."

All six people in the room stopped talking and spun toward us in unison.

"Nonna!" shrieked the little girls. "Where did you and Lea go? Did you get captured?"

Lea and Mrs. Zola shared an uneasy look, but the older woman didn't answer.

"Where have you been?" Mattias demanded. "I come home, and you're not here."

"Where did *you* go?" asked his wife. "Four hours we're waiting for you, and no word. Lea and I went to check the garage, and there was no one there."

"That's because I went to the church first. Father Deflorio and I were looking for Michael—ah! You found him!"

"I—uh—" I wasn't really sure what to say here.

"Good." Lea's brother shoved between his grand-parents. "I want to give this asshole a piece of my mind.

You think you can mess with my sister and get away with it, Scarrone? No fuckin' way."

"Oh my God, *stop!*" Lea snapped at Matthew as she parried his hand out of the way and stepped in front of me. "Watch your mouth around the kids, huh? And no one asked you to stick your big nose in here. I don't need your protection, *Matthew*. Especially not from Michael."

But I was stepping in front of her before she could continue, standing up to my full height. I wasn't the tallest man in the room—Matthew had me by a couple of inches—but I was the biggest. "It's all right, Tess. I can take a few punches."

"Tess?" Matthew repeated. "That's not your name. And what the hell happened to your face?"

I touched the cut above my eye that had finally stopped bleeding but was probably still ugly to look at. All of me would be a mess of bruises in the morning. Not that I had any regrets.

"It's short for contessa," I said with a quick glance at Lea that made her cheeks turn pink. "It's because she's regal. Like a queen. At least to me."

Every single one of Lea's sisters squealed in unison. But I wasn't the slightest bit embarrassed when Lea took my hand back and squeezed it really tight.

"Nonna and I were taken to Morrisania," Lea said. "Some bad dudes were looking for Michael and thought I would make good bait. Nonna got caught up because she was with me too."

"What?!" Mattia's face swung toward me, full of anger all over again. "You put my wife and grand-daughter into danger? How dare you—"

"Mattias, stop." Sofia Zola's voice brooked no argument, and her husband, almost like a child, immediately quieted. "He is a good boy. He should *not* have been in Lea's room, but it's not his fault these bad men wanted to find him. He loves her. I saw it myself. He fought too many men to protect her, to protect me. He was ready to give his life for her."

"He wasn't the only one willing to do that," Lea said, chin lifted in defiance.

Yeah, we'd be having words about that later. I wasn't too happy about her little stunt when Ricky got that gun.

But my girl was valiant like a lion. I couldn't exactly fault her for that. Especially when I knew it only came from love.

I looked back at Matthew, then at Mattias, standing behind him. Both men seemed to be processing what we were all trying to tell them. But I realized there was one thing I hadn't said. Maybe the most important thing of all.

"Look," I said, then swallowed hard, trying to gather my words together. Trying to do this justice. "I would have taken a bullet for her if it meant getting her and your wife out of that room, Mattias. I would have given my life and then some. I honestly can't think of a better way to go."

I swallowed hard. This wasn't about what happened in Morrisania. I needed to get to the heart of things.

"I could say a lot of things about what happened last night and today," I said. "And I will. I'll tell you whatever you want to hear. But it all comes down to this: I love your granddaughter more than anything. I haven't had a lot of good luck, and God knows I've made some mistakes. Never had a family like yours, never had anyone to care for me like she does, never anyone who inspired me to be better. But she does all of that and more. And I...I finally see a reason to be around. All I want is to spend forever trying to make sure Lea has the best life possible. We love each other. That's all there is to it."

I looked around, expecting arguments. Waiting for Mattias to take a swing at me or kick me out of his house.

No one spoke for what seemed like minutes. Even the little girls on the sofa were watching their grandfather warily, like they knew my little speech would either make him melt or blow up completely.

"*Dai*, Mattias, the boy saved our lives today!" Mrs. Zola finally spoke. "Let him in so he can get warm, at least, eh? He's a part of the family now. We might as well get him some food too."

She grabbed her husband's coat and yanked it off him in order to hang it up. The movement seemed to wake everyone up.

"All right," he said with another wary, if more accepting glance my way despite the fact that his wife was now towing him toward the kitchen. "One drink. And then we gonna set some ground rules for the two of you."

"Close the door, Lea," Nonna ordered. "You're letting in all the cold air. Girls, come help to make dinner, okay?"

"Nonna, are there anything leftovers from last night?" Matthew could be heard asking as he followed everyone out of the room. "All this fighting makes me hungry."

"Mattie, are you ever not hungry?" Kate wondered.

After she closed the door, Lea and I turned to face each other, suddenly left with a moment alone as her family disappeared down the hallway.

For a moment, we blinked at each other in a daze. I couldn't blame her. The whole afternoon seemed like a dream.

Then we launched at each other, equally wrapped up in a need to reconnect.

"You stupid man," she said in between ferocious kisses. "What the hell were you doing getting involved with those guys?"

"I was trying to get out," I told her, though I couldn't quite stop sucking on her bottom lip. "They were loose ends. From before, you know?"

We kissed again, this time only stopping once we both seemed to realize that anyone from her family could walk in on us again and then we'd really be screwed.

I set her away from me, and she didn't argue. Her green eyes sparkled with the same adoration I was sure was pasted all over my face.

I felt warm. Energized, but not in a hurry. Ready for whatever might come, but equally happy to stay right here forever.

Safety, I realized. That's what that feeling was. And I was experiencing it for the very first time, right here, with her.

"Don't you ever do that to me again," I whispered, framing her face with my hands.

Unable to help myself, I pressed another, more gentle kiss on her full lips.

Lea smiled against my mouth. "We should clean up your face."

"Later," I said before kissing her again.

But she had something on her mind. "So, that man...the one who said you owe him a favor..."

I shook my head. "I don't think that will matter anytime soon. Lis Antoni respects integrity. He'll wait for me to come to him."

Lea didn't look so sure. "You promise."

I smoothed back her hair from her face so I could see her clearly. "On my honor. Which you know belongs to you."

Her grin about split my chest in two. "Because you love me?"

I nodded. "And because you love me."

Then I kissed her again, and this time, I didn't stop for a good long while.

Sometime later, we finally broke apart, and Lea looked me up and down with lust in her slightly open mouth and love in her eyes.

"We need to find you an apartment," she said emphatically. "There is no *way* Nonno is going to let me work at the garage anymore without him around."

I chuckled, even though she was undoubtedly right. Last night was only the beginning for us, and I wanted to do a hell of a lot more than kiss Lea right now.

But not here. Her grandfather was inviting me into his house, and her grandmother had just called me family, but that didn't mean we were totally in the clear. I had a long way to go to earn the man's trust. To my surprise, I was looking forward to the process. It was something to aspire to. Something I really wanted.

"I'll get a room somewhere close by," I told her. "But honestly, it doesn't matter where I live, Tess."

Lea frowned. "Why do you say that?"

I smiled. "Because no matter what, you'll always be home to me."

EPILOGUE

DON'T MAKE ME CRY...OR MAYBE DO

February 2002

Lea

"I now pronounce you husband and wife."

A cheer rose in the little chapel of Our Redeemer, rising through the arches over the nave and aisles while Michael and I took our first kiss as a married couple. It was almost appropriate for a church.

Almost.

Married. Holy crap.

Everyone outside the Zola household had said we were crazy. My friends couldn't believe that at nineteen, only halfway through my first year of college at Fordham, I was already someone's wife. I wouldn't have believed it myself, except for the fact that it was literally the only thing I had wanted with this man since nearly the moment I'd met him.

Inside the house, I had a sneaking suspicion that by the end of the year, my grandparents wanted nothing more than for Michael to put a ring on my finger and make an honest woman out of me. We hadn't taken advantage of their home again, but my grandparents weren't stupid. After all, they themselves got married even younger for probably the exact same reasons.

My only regret was that we hadn't done it sooner. I would have liked my nonno to walk me down the aisle instead of my brother. Instead, we had lost him four months earlier. When he was diagnosed with cancer, the doctors gave him two months to live. He made it six. But the last few were particularly hard.

Michael, however, was there the whole time. After moving into a shared apartment a few blocks south, he took on a more active role at the shop, stepping in to help with the books and eventually taking over all of the driving business once Nonno got too sick to be behind the wheel. All the while, he insisted I stay in college instead of taking a year off like I suggested. When I was awarded a full academic scholarship to Fordham, Michael was the one who hooted like the wolf and shouted it out the window so the whole neighborhood knew.

I couldn't waste an opportunity like that, he insisted. Whatever I needed, he would be there, whether that meant sitting up with me to finish papers when I was too overcome with grief to focus or taking care of my sisters here and there so I could have extra time to study.

My man proved that he was really and truly a part of the family, again and again. Which was why, I supposed, when we told everyone we wanted to get married, we barely heard an argument. It was just making official what we already knew to be true. Michael's last name was Scarrone, but he'd always be a Zola.

IT WASN'T A BIG RECEPTION. Just a little party at Tino's restaurant, which my grandfather's best friend had offered to us to celebrate, complete with home-made pasta on the house for the forty or so friends and family who came and, of course, my favorite tiramisu. Nonno's picture hung next to us at our table, a hole we'd never be able to fill, but no one would want to anyway.

There were toasts and cheers, and even a few envelopes of cash slid in our direction. But at the end of the night, Michael and I found ourselves wrapped in each other's arms in the corner, completely wrapped up in each other as Frank Sinatra crooned "All the Way" over the speakers. I admired the little diamond ring I discovered that Michael had put on layaway the week after he first said, "I love you." Michael just admired me and whispered sweet and decidedly naughty ideas of what he wanted to do to his wife in my ear.

"Ahem."

Michael and I turned at the sound of my brother's voice, but my husband didn't let me go. He didn't have to anymore, and I could tell he was taking full advantage.

"Hey, Matt," he said as he slid me in front of him,

keeping his hands firmly at my waist. "What's up, man?"

Matthew shifted uneasily from foot to foot and cleared his throat awkwardly. "I—sorry to interrupt."

"It's no problem," I said but frowned when I caught his eyes glistening again. "What is it?"

"I—I didn't have the guts to do this in front of everyone. Nonno would have wanted it that way. You remember he would have made a big speech congratulating you two and everything." Matthew emitted a wry chuckle. "He liked you in the end, Mike. Told me that himself."

Michael's arms around me tightened. "Yeah?"

"Yeah. It's why…" Matthew shook his head, clearly overcome by emotion. "It's why he told me that when he was gone, and if you ever got married, he wanted me to give you this. For the two of you."

Tears welled up in my own eyes when I took the envelope Matthew was holding; our names scratched across the front. I'd thought I'd seen the last of Nonno's familiar scrawl.

Michael's arms remained strong around my waist as he set his chin on my shoulder. "Go on, Tess. Open it."

So I did.

Inside the envelope were a bunch of documents, too many to look through at one time.

"What is this?" I asked.

"It's the papers to the shop," Matthew said. "He wanted you to have it. You and Mike."

My eyes flew over the ownership papers, underneath them a copy of Nonno's will clearly stating that when he died, the entirety of his estate would pass to his beloved wife, but for one exception: in the event of my marriage to one Michael Scarrone, Zola Auto and Drive would go to us as a wedding gift.

"I don't think he imagined it would be this soon." Matthew quirked a sardonic black brow. "Jesus, Le, you're still a teenager, you know?"

I chuckled, then looked at Nonna, who was still wearing all black in honor of her husband, even while enjoying her third glass of wine. When Michael and I had told her that we wanted to get married only one year after we first met, I had expected more of an argument from her.

But to my surprise, she'd only said one thing: "When you know, you know."

"So were they," I said. "And they were the happiest couple in the world. When you know, you know."

Michael's laughter was a low rumble against my chest before he pressed a kiss to my cheek. "I always knew."

I twisted to look at him. "Me too."

Matthew watched our interaction, his eyes glazed a little at the memory of our grandfather. Out of all of us, he'd been taking the loss of Nonno the hardest. Had even taken to wearing Nonno's old hats, as if they helped him live up to becoming the new man of the house. On top of that, he'd started attending Mass weekly beside Nonna, and I'd caught him saying his rosaries multiple times a week.

Survivor's guilt was a powerful thing. I wondered if my poor brother would ever be able to shake it for good.

"But what about you?" I asked, suddenly aware that

we were the only ones benefiting from the will. "Shouldn't this belong to all six of us? I don't want to take this away from you and the girls. Not to mention Nonna."

But Matthew shook his head. "I won't be around in another eighteen months. It wouldn't make sense for me to take over just to leave again. And he made sure Nonna was taken care of."

A shadow seemed to fall across the room. At Christmas, my brother announced his plans to join the Marines after he graduated from college and go to officer training. I didn't know if it was a reaction to 9/11 or Nonno's death a few weeks after, but his resolve was clear: he could do more with his life fighting for what was right than taking some white-collar job out of school.

The response hadn't been great. Marie and Joni had immediately started crying after someone told them what the Marines were, Frankie ran upstairs and refused to come back down, Kate had started railing about the military industrial complex, and Nonna had shouted things in Italian that made all of our faces turn red.

In the end, it was Michael who returned Christmas morning to a state of relative calm. He had quickly and quietly ushered Matthew out of the house for a talk, man to man, asking Nonna and me to work on breakfast so that when they got back, everyone could eat and we could have this conversation without the added stress of empty stomachs.

When they came back, Matthew's decision hadn't changed, but I could tell he was taking the effect on us more seriously, which made the rest of us more willing to listen. It was the first time I saw Michael step into the role that I had a feeling Nonno had always seen. A quiet leader among men. Smart and capable. Someone we could all trust to come through in times of trouble.

I shook my head. I refused to let that particular raincloud ruin this day.

Michael's arms gave my waist another squeeze. "We can talk about that tomorrow," he said to both of us. "For now... thank you, man. This is too much."

Matthew shook his head. "It's exactly right. You're the man for the job, Mike. You and Lea—you're what will hold this family together. It's exactly what he wanted."

I folded the papers back into the envelope, then stepped forward to wrap my arms around my brother's neck. "Love you, big brother."

He squeezed me back and kissed me on the cheek. "Love you too, you pain in the ass."

He and Michael gave each other an obligatory fist bump that somehow turned into a brief hug before Matthew disappeared back into the crowd, probably to find Sherry. I wasn't sure if he had told her about his new plans, but I doubted she was happy. As much as I didn't like the girl, at least I'd have an ally in keeping my brother home.

"Hey."

Michael's fingers slid under my chin, tugging me around to face him. "You okay?"

I nodded, then slid my arms around his shoulders. "I'm good. Great, even. It's just weird. I was thinking about how weddings are so...final. I know the only thing that's changed is this ring on my finger, but it seemed like something was ending. I can't figure out how. Or whether I should be happy or sad about it."

Michael examined me for a long moment, then seemed to come to a conclusion. "Come with me."

"Where are we going?" I demanded as he grabbed our coats off a nearby table, then tugged me toward the kitchen entrance instead of the main exit. "People are going to wonder where we've gone. They're going to want to wish us goodbye!"

"They'll survive," Michael said as we wound our way around the dishwasher. "But I won't. And I have something to show you."

"What's that?"

"Not an ending. Call it a new beginning."

WE WALKED THROUGH BELMONT, enjoying the familiar sights and sounds of the neighborhood. In the last year, I'd only become more aware of how much the neighborhood could change. Nonno's death had fallen like one of a long line of dominoes, as several of his old friends had left the neighborhood in the last year, especially after 9/11. New York as a whole was changing in the face of the disaster. In some ways, the city was bonding together like it never had. In others, it was splintering more than over.

Michael turned down Lorillard Place, and we walked up a few more blocks until we were passing the park and the parish school for Our Redeemer on the other side.

"We all went to school there," I said, pointing across the tennis courts. "I always thought I'd send my kids there one day too. The nuns were actually pretty nice."

Michael gave me a funny look. "I remember. You told me that over the summer."

He came to a stop, his expression suddenly solemn. His eyes traveled over my entire body, from the hair I'd curled under the white fascinator borrowed from Nonna to the tea-length white dress Kate had helped me find at one of her favorite vintage shops to the blue heels I'd found at the mall on sale.

"You're so beautiful," he murmured. "And all mine."

"Is everything okay?" I asked. "What's going on?"

Michael took a deep breath and exhaled into the cold night air. "Mattias gave me something else before he died. He gave me some money. Told me he was proud of me and that he wanted me to go make myself a life so I could welcome you into it."

I blinked away another round of tears. "You never told me that."

Michael shrugged, that shy, bashful movement that had come to signal when he was uncomfortable with doing something right or noble. "He asked me not to. He wanted it to be my accomplishment, not his."

Then he turned halfway toward the building. "What do you think?"

The two-story house wasn't exactly pretty. The blue paint was peeling on the outside, worse on the bay window, where the white trim was completely chipped off the bottom sill. The railing looked like it was about to fall over, and the window on the second floor looked cracked in multiple places.

But it was a house. A real house in the neighborhood where I had grown up.

"Did you buy this?" It was honestly hard to believe, considering he had been homeless a year ago.

Michael shook his head. "Not yet, but I will eventually. I made a deal with the owner—rent to buy. But if the shop keeps doing well, maybe we can get a real mortgage in a few more years. What do you think?"

I stared up at the building, unable to answer. Barely even able to think.

Whatever I was expecting him to show me tonight, it was not this.

"I can fix the stuff that's wrong," Michael rattled on as he looked with me. "I did a good job helping Mattias fix that plumbing problem at your house, remember? And now that he taught me how to put up drywall, I can redo the upstairs bedroom, like next week if we want. The kitchen's a little rough, but I think you can use it until we save up for something nicer." He stopped, watching me like I was a bomb about to go off. "Please, Tess. Say something. If you're gonna yell at me, then do it. But I need to know what you think."

Finally, I found my voice. "This is *amazing*."

His dark eyes, framed with those impossibly thick lashes, sparked in the night. "Yeah?"

I nodded. "Just when I think you can't surprise me, you go and do something like this."

He bit back a smile but couldn't hide his dimples. "I'm glad you like it, baby girl. I got it for you. For us."

I looked back at it, appraising. "It's definitely got

potential. But I don't think that we should start with the bedroom. The kitchen is the heart of the home, so really that's what we should tackle firs—whaa!"

I shrieked as my husband literally swept me off my feet princess-style and proceeded to carry me up the short flight of steps.

"Gotta fix that loose step," he noted as he skipped a particularly crooked one. "Do me a favor and get the keys out of my pocket?"

"You are ridiculous," I said, twisting around to fish his keys from the left side of his coat.

I sat back up to find that sooty gaze fixed on me with so much love that I thought my heart might burst.

"Ridiculously in love with you," he said, then pressed a kiss to my lips. "And if you thought I wasn't going to carry my wife across the threshold of our new house, you're kidding yourself. Open it up."

He held me still while I unlocked the door. It swung open, revealing a homely living room with battered parquet floors. The only furniture in the room was a mattress I recognized from the room Michael had been renting for the past year, made up with soft white bedding and rose petals scattered over the top. Otherwise, the only other items in the room were too many candles to count, all flickering brightly through the darkness.

"Wow," I breathed, still safe in his arms. "Michael Scarrone. I had no idea you were such a romantic."

He nuzzled my ear, humming with contentment.

"A little romance to carry my bride across our new threshold seemed like the right thing to do," he said before kissing me thoroughly enough that I lost my breath completely. "Now, let's go inside. I want to welcome home my contessa."

THE END…OR IS IT?

Thank you so much for reading Lea and Michael's sweet story! This is a standalone prequel to a much bigger series following all of the Zola sisters.

Joni's story is next, taking place 18 years later! You can preorder her standalone fake-relationship, roommates-to-lovers romance here: www.nicolefrenchro mance.com/boyfriendofthehour

If you want more of the Zola family right now, here are a few complete stories already available:

First Comes Love
When British chef Xavier Parker returns to New York looking for Francesca Zola five years after they had one hot month, he isn't expecting to meet a little girl who looks just like him. Or to discover his former lover had his daughter and never told him…
Read it here: www.nicolefrenchromance.com/first comeslove

The Other Man
After sharing a single night with an elegant mystery woman, Matthew Zola has been searching for his dream girl for months. When he finally finds her, he

discovers that she is married…and her husband is the monster Matthew is trying to put behind bars.

Read it here: www.nicolefrenchromance.com/first comeslove

Keep reading for a FREE SAMPLE of First Comes Love!

ACKNOWLEDGMENTS

Sometimes you think you're going to write a story, and then another one pops up in your head. And then you think you're going to write that one as a short novella, and it turns out to be more than sixty thousand words.

Things change, is what I'm saying, and I'm never more grateful for the team of supporters behind me than when these characters start talking and I have no choice but to obey.

So now that you have enjoyed this story, please join me in gratitutde for the following wonderful people:

My alpha readers—Patricia, Dawn, Kymberly, and Lacie—thank you for picking up and putting down whatever I'm writing at a moments notice and answering my messages even after two weeks. You are such wonderful, joyous readers. I love you all.

My assistant, Danielle, who always scrambles whenever I ask, even if it's at ten o'clock the night before a release. Not necessary, but always appreciated. Your love for this industry is inspiring.

My publicist and rights agent, Dani Sanchez, for brainstorming all things marketing and allowing me to change release schedules more times than I can count. You are a treasure.

To Theresa Leigh and Marla Esposito for being

available on the last of the last notice. I could not have done this without you. The pig is more like Miss Piggy now. I am so eternally grateful.

To my other author friends who allow me to complain every day and also join me whenever I'm happy: Laura, Jane, Claudia, Parker, and many more. I appreciate you all so much

And of course, to The Dude and Kid French. Thank you for allowing me to hibernate for weekends at a time to finish this bish, and also just for being the best family a girl could want. I love you both with my whole heart and soul.

ABOUT THE AUTHOR

Nicole French is a lifelong dreamer, low-key fashion addict, and total bookworm. When not writing fiction or secretly reading gossip columns, she is hanging out with her family or going on dates with her husband. In her spare time, she likes to go running or practice the piano, but never seems to do either one of these things as much as she should.

For more information about Nicole French and to keep informed about upcoming releases, please:

Visit her website at www.nicolefrenchromance.com/.

Check out Nicole's Goodreads page: www.goodreads.com/authornicolefrench

Want to hook up with other Nicole French readers or interact with the author? Join Nicole's reader group, La Merde.

www.ingramcontent.com/pod-product-compliance
Lightning Source LLC
Chambersburg PA
CBHW030327200626
46816CB00006BA/1963